I0628085

Brooklyn On Lock

Sonovia Alexander

Lock Down Publications

Presents

Brooklyn On Lock

A Novel by *Sonovia Alexander*

Sonovia Alexander

Lock Down Publications
P.O. Box 1482
Pine Lake, Ga 30072-1482

Copyright 2015 by Sonovia Alexander Brooklyn On Lock

All rights reserved. No part of this book may be reproduced in any form or by electronic or mechanical means, including information storage and retrieval systems without permission in writing from the publisher, except by a reviewer who may quote brief passages in review.
First Edition July 2015
Printed in the United States of America

This is a work of fiction. Names, characters, places, and incidents either are products of the author's imagination or are used fictitiously. Any similarity to actual events or locales or persons, living or dead, is entirely coincidental.

Lock Down Publications
Facebook: Sonovia Walker-Alexander
Like our page on Facebook: Lock Down Publications @
www.facebook.com/lockdownpublications.ldp
Cover design and layout by: **Dynasty's Cover Me**
Book interior design by: **Shawn Walker**
Edited by: **Eartha Watts-Hicks**

This book is dedicated to each of my supporters.

Thank you!

Sonovia Alexander

Prologue

Boom! Boom! Boom! Boom!

Taz B let off four shots, gripping his .45 in his hand as he ran through the projects, trying to reach his building. He ducked as bullets whizzed past his head and kept running until he reached the entrance.

Ron D saw people he recognized chasing Taz B from Marcus Garvey Houses. Ron now pulled out his 9mm and fired shots of his own. "I got you covered, Taz! Get in the building!" Ron D screamed, as he kept firing shots at the three people he could see who were dressed in all black attire. They were running letting off shots as they ducked around cars that were parked in front of the buildings.

Taz B entered the building. It was too early in the morning he thought for him to be running from neighborhood thugs that were out looking for trouble. Taz B yanked the door open leading to the stairwell, ran up four flights of stairs and kept running until he reached his apartment. Fumbling with his keys, he unlocked the door and hurried inside. Behind his locked door, he stood panting until he caught his breath. His brother, Mo, rushed out of his room when he heard the door slam. Mo had a frown on his face wondering why his brother was making a racket upon entering their home.

Trying to steady his heart rate, Taz B remained by the door with his gun pointed towards the floor. Taz B's feet were hurting from running in his work boots. This gun battle in warm weather had sweat beads dotting his forehead. This was supposed to be a normal day, and that morning, Taz was just coming in from working his overnight shift.

Shocked, Mo needed an explanation. "What the fuck just happened?" Mo stared at his brother, still with the warm gun in his hand.

"Those motherfuckers from Garvey projects just started popping off on me, so I returned fire. They chased me all the way here. I know I caught one. I saw him drop. I do not know who these motherfuckers are or why they shot at me, but they will get what is coming to them. I do not fuck with anyone and I have been walking that way from work after getting off the L train for months. I never had this problem before," Taz B explained, unbuttoning the neck of his work shirt. For a few years, he had kept his hands clean from selling drugs or anything else illegal. There was no reason for any local niggas to fuck with him, since he was no longer in the game.

Mo took the gun from his brother's hand. He then grabbed his jacket and said, "Stay here and keep an eye on Mommy. I'll be right back." Running down the staircase, he tucked the gun at the small of his back and skipped steps.

Mo could not understand why niggas in the hood always seemed to try to get at his family. Niggas knew that Mo was not to be fucked with, those that knew him well. He had already proven to some that he was certifiably crazy long ago. He had killed two cops and gotten off. And the murder weapon, that could have possibly put Mo away for a very, long time, was never found. Witnesses were too afraid to testify. Mo had also thrown a person off the roof of a 5-story building. The person had made the mistake of breaking into their home and stealing their mother's jewelry. There had never been a time that anyone would have enough courage to go up against him. With all the stories going around the hood about Mo, most of the dudes his age were afraid of him. That was in Mo's teen years, but upon Mo's return to his Brownsville neighborhood, he noticed that the streets were flooded with young boys playing the grown man's game. Mo understood that some of these young dudes did not know about him. Mo really tried to keep to himself and mind his business. He did not feel the need to live his life the same way he did in his past. He had so much more to live for now.

Mo was only 28 years old. He stood 5 foot 11 inches tall. He was about 200lbs but all muscles. He was dark skinned with dreads that he kept neatly tied back in a ponytail. Women (who were not too afraid of him) threw themselves at him all the time because of his light brown eyes. Mo had his main girl, Bella, who was his ride or die…for real. She held him down, like no other.

Mo had been the family protector for many years now. He now adjusted the waistband of his pants to better conceal the gun tucked away at the small of his back and headed downstairs. Mo thought for a moment of how different life would be for him and his family had his father still been around. He wanted so much to go back to the life he had started and he had come accustomed to before moving back to Brownsville. He and his brother Taz B both had bettered their situations once they left home. Unfortunately, after receiving a phone call from their mother in late November, they returned to be with her.

Taz B was 22 years old. He was 6 foot tall and had a caramel complexion like their mother. He was 225 pounds solid, mostly because of his height. Taz B's dreads were not as long as Mo's, but he was just as fine as his older brother was. The youngest of the brothers was T Ski. T Ski was 15 years old. He was about 5 feet 7 inches tall. He was the quiet one. He also inherited the caramel complexion from his mother. Mo was the only one that was dark, like their father who was incarcerated. T Ski was a skinny and average looking boy. He weighed about 145 lbs. He mostly stayed in the house, once he arrived home from school. He also had dreads. Everyone knew who the brothers were. They all looked alike and possessed the same attitude. Although T Ski was quiet, he had gotten into plenty of fights in school and had even broken a kid's arm after hitting him with a chair. Being that T Ski was a quiet and very intelligent, boy that never troubled his teachers, unlike his adversary; he didn't get in trouble for it.

Evelyn, their mother, was 46 years old. She was diagnosed with an incurable disease. After six months of tests, doctors still had not pinpointed out what it was. Evelyn had gone into work in late November and had fallen ill. Her coworker had escorted her to the hospital. She had all kinds of test run on her and the results showed that she had an uncommon disease that had no cure like Cancer. Evelyn was a beautiful woman. She was 5 foot 6 inches tall with dreads down the middle of her back. She kept them neat and fashionable. Her gold locks complimented her golden complexion. She had long eyelashes and a mole that was above her lip. She had a body to die for still at her age. She was so happy and full of life, before she was diagnosed with her sickness. She no longer had the will to live anymore. Her husband was in jail doing 25 years in which he had served 10 of those years. She did not want to go through this alone. She stopped going to the doctor because she wanted to die. Mo and Taz B had moved back home to help take care of their mother. Mo thought that if he could convince his mother to go back to another doctor for a second opinion, they would surely be able to find out what her diagnosis was. Evelyn did not feel the same way. Ultimately, they did not force her to go to the hospital, nor did they force her to take medication. They loved their mother and wanted to respect her wishes but were not going to allow her to take her own life.

They all honored their parents' wishes for them to go to school and get educated. Andrea was 19 and away in college. She was Evelyn's only girl. Andrea had not been home since she went off to college a year ago. She had gotten a job. She was 5 foot 4 inches tall with hazel eyes and a high yellow complexion. She was bowlegged and the men went crazy over that. She had small breast. A plump ass made up for it. Andrea was not aware of her mother's condition. None of the boys bothered to tell her. Mo did not want his sister having a reason to leave college and come home. He hated her being in Brooklyn anyway. Niggas on the street knew that Andrea was his heart and they always tried their hands by talking to Andrea. It was Mo's idea for her to attend college outside of New York. Once she was off, Mo was relieved. Mo wanted to get his mother out of the projects and give her the life that she deserved, but she refused to leave. She had been born and raised in Brownsville, and she said that she was going to die in Brownsville.

Evelyn's sister Sheryl came by once a week to give the boys a break. She would stay with her sister the whole day and talk with her. Every time Sheryl would go visit her sister, she could see Evelyn getting weaker and slipping away. Their mother Vanda was old and couldn't get around much. She didn't even know how badly her daughter's health had deteriorated. The family kept that secret to avoid upsetting Vanda. They had a big family, and they were all spread throughout Brooklyn.

T Ski was always in his room working on things. No one knew exactly what he would be doing because of the locks that he kept on his door. He was very private and his family respected that. Mo was their protector and provider. One thing that made these boys different then all of the others in the hood, they had a desire to make something of themselves and not let where they were from be an excuse to keep them down. Mo had a Bachelor Degree in Business but worked in a law firm as an accountant. He had taken a leave of absence from work to cater more to Evelyn. Some days she would be okay. Others she looked like she was about to leave this world. Taz B had his Associate's degree in Business, as well and was taking online classes working towards his Bachelor. His occupation was in hotel management.

***

Mo walked out of the building and looked around. He saw guys running toward Marcus Garvey projects. He made a mental note of the clothing they were wearing. Mo checked his surroundings, once again before going back inside the building. He then pulled out his two-way pager and sent a "411" message to one of his boys for info. He needed to know who exactly was after his brother and why.

Mo hated Brooklyn but knew that as long as his mother was here, he wasn't going anywhere. As he turned to walk back inside he ran into Ron D.

"Sugar Foot sent his people." Ron D said. As they crossed paths, he gave Mo dap, and kept on walking. Ron D was heading to the back of the building to meet up with a dope fiend. He knew it wouldn't be long before Mo showed up to find out what was going on with his brother. Ron D was a short brown skin guy that stayed fly. He loved his Jordan sneakers and was the first in the hood to get the newest ones as soon as they reached the stores. He was nice looking with a low fade and a goatee that he sported on his face. Ron D and Mo were close and tight when it came down to handling business. They never talked aloud. They would mention names of the

14

ringleaders they had beef with or they would drop the project name just in case anyone was within earshot.

Mo knew that since his own name held weight here in the streets, no matter how hard he fought to walk the straight and narrow; niggas were going to continually test him. He was still that nigga that was not to be fucked with. Mo hated dealing with the bullshit that came along with living in the hood. There was always a dude in the hood looking for a come up. Robbing innocent people, killing innocent people, and just bringing heat to the hood just because they wanted to make a name for themselves. He wished his mother would leave this place, but she refused.

Sonovia Alexander

Chapter 1
Tilden High School
May 14, 2005

"Thank you for coming in. I have been trying to reach Terence's parents for months. Are you his father?" Principal Edmonds asked Mo.

"No. I'm his older brother Montague. Is he in trouble?" Mo asked.

"No. Do you know that your brother was tested in the beginning of the school year? His academic level being above average, he was given an IQ test. He scored 150, which classifies him as a genius. We then had a licensed proctor come in to further test. Terence was given the Mensa Workout, which is an aptitude test administered for entrance into a society of individuals whose IQs range in the top 2 percentile. And like I said, he scored…high. We have been waiting to meet with one of his parents to push him further ahead, because our curriculum is not challenging enough for him. The board of education believes that it might be more of a challenge to him by taking the proper test to see if he could be placed in a college. I have scheduled an appointment for him to be taken to meet with this association," Principal Edmonds handed Mo a card and a folder with paper work for Mo to fill out to take with him. "Please, take him there. Your brother is very special, and we want to see him…reach his full potential in a setting more suitable. Would your mother be able to go along with him? After meeting with the associates, the forms would need to be filled out by his guardian to disenrollment him from this school."

Mo took the card and put it in his pocket. He went through the folder scanning the contents inside. He closed the folder back and held it in his hand. "My mother is ill. The doctors have stated that she is dealing with something that's terminal. We don't know how long she would have with us so if anything, I would be handling anything dealing with my brother. Thank you for bringing this to my attention." Mo shook the principal's hand and walked out of the office.

T Ski waited out in the hallway for his brother, wondering if something was going on at home. The office clerk hadn't discussed with him why he was being pulled from class. The only thing that was stated was his brother was here to pick him up. T Ski thought that he had done something wrong. He waited until he saw his brother Mo walk out of the office. T Ski grabbed his belongings and walked off with his brother, heading for home.

Tilden Projects

The ride from the school to their home was short and Mo was reticent. He unlocked the door to their apartment and walked inside. T Ski was close behind. Lost in his own thoughts, the teen went straight for his bedroom, closing and locking the door behind him.

Mo couldn't believe what he had been told earlier. Mo walked to his mother's bedroom and went inside. Evelyn was sitting up in the bed looking out of the window. This was something she would do from time to time when alone. She turned her head toward the door when she heard someone enter the room. She looked at her eldest son and smiled. Mo moved toward the side of her bed to retrieve the tray of food he had fed her before he left for T Ski's school and placed the empty tray on her dresser closest to the door. He didn't want to forget to take it out with him.

Every morning Mo would open the curtains to allow some light shine into the room, since his mother spent most of her days staring toward the window. Her room was decorated in light colors, which made the room feel comfortable. It felt peaceful every time Mo set foot inside his mother room. Evelyn watched her son move about in her room.

Mo walked over to her, leaned down, and kissed her on the forehead. He pulled the nearest chair up next to her bed. Mo sat down and buried his face in his hands. He didn't know how he was going to get his mother to understand that she had given birth to a genius. They all knew that T Ski was ascetic and stayed experimenting.

"Mom, I just left T Ski's school. They say that he's a genius." Evelyn looked at her son with wide eyes. She then turned to face the window again. Mo wondered what was going through his mother mind right now. She looked as if she is in good spirits today, seemed that when he left the home, she was lying down and now she was sitting up staring out of the window from her bed. Mo shook his head. He wished his mother would snap out of this state of mind she was in. He hated seeing her like this knowing that the days were numbered. Mo wished that she would live out the rest of her days being happy.

Mo looked out the window, as he reclined back in the chair he was sitting in. He was trying to find the right words to say to his brother. He could hardly believe it himself. He had never known of anyone else with an IQ that high. Mo sat a while longer with his mother before he got up and walked out of her room. He went straight to T Ski's room. Mo knocked on the door. He waited for an answer. T Ski unlocked the door and slightly opened it.

20

"What's up?" T Ski asked, peaking his head through the door.

"I need to talk to you about something important." Mo said in a stern tone. T Ski was about to shut the door when Mo put his foot inside to prevent him from closing it. "I want to come inside your room to talk to you." T Ski looked at Mo and knew that he was serious. T Ski opened the door and let Mo inside.

Mo couldn't remember the last time he set foot inside his brother's room. He was in awe at the sight in front of him. He knew that everything the principal had told him was in fact true. His brother was a genius. It looked like a science lab in his brother's room. He had different chemicals in flasks. There were also telescopes, scales, a table, and more. Mo looked at his brother. "Your principal told me that you were a genius today." T Ski looked at his brother and walked over to the window.

"I know what I am," T Ski responded.

"Why didn't you tell anyone? Do you know where you could be right now? What's holding you here, T, with all the intelligence you possess?" Mo questioned.

"I don't need to tell you what's holding me here. I'm not going anywhere. I don't belong around all of those people in corporate America. I'm not one of them. I'm a hood nigga just like you are," T Ski said, looking back out of his window.

"You are dead wrong about that little brother. We might live in the hood, but we are far from hood niggas. We're educated and strong black men, raised by a strong queen and king. We have good things going on in our lives in spite of the street life. But you can do something great with your intelligence. You need to utilize it and get the hell out of here. You can invent anything and make millions," Mo said with excitement in his voice.

"I have been working on something and I want you to try it out. I was going to wait until I was sure about the product."

Mo looked at his brother with a raised brow. "What do you mean by product? Show me what you're talking about." T Ski walked over to what he called his lab and put on his safety goggles. Mo crossed his arms over his chest and waited patiently to see what his brother was up to.

"Try this," T Ski said, as he held up a tea spoon filled with white liquid. Mo looked at him like he was crazy.

"What the hell is that?" Mo said, as he took the spoon.

"Try it and let me know what you think." Mo raised the spoon to his mouth and drank the contents. T Ski looked at Mo and waited.

"It tastes nasty. What is it?" Mo asked, as he wiped his mouth with the back of his hand.

22

"Give it a minute, and let me know how you feel." T Ski grabbed a bottle of liquid from his dresser and put it on his table. He then grabbed a bottle of water and put some of the contents from the bottle inside of the water bottle. He looked over at Mo and laughed to himself. Mo was quiet and had a blank stare on his face. T Ski gave him the water to drink. Mo didn't want the water. He pushed T Ski's hand away. T Ski put the bottle to Mo's lips and made him drink it. A few seconds later, Mo started blinking his eyes.

"What the hell was that you gave me? That shit had me stuck on stupid and horny at the same time. I felt myself getting a hard on, and I was feeling like I smoked 10 bags of weed," Mo said with slurred words.

T Ski laughed because he knew that if it worked, that was the effect he was looking for. "It's something I made. I call it K2O."

Mo was starting to feel like himself again. "What the fuck did you just give me? That shit was good. The taste, I wasn't too thrilled about, but that shit made me feel good. Had you not given me that water to drink, how long would I have been like that."

"I need you to find me a crack head and bring them here. I need you to give it to them and see how long it will last before they want more," T Ski said, while he started mixing up something else.

Mo looked at his brother like he was crazy. "I know you didn't just say something stupid like that out of your mouth. For you to think for one second that I would invite a fiend into this house to sample something you created, you must really think that I have stupid written across my forehead. That's out of the fucking question." Mo felt his temper rising. He didn't know why his brother thought that he would allow something like that to take place where they lay their heads.

"I need to see how long this will last. Why don't you call Travis over and have him sample this," T Ski suggested.

"I just told you that isn't fucking happening. This is what you want to use your intelligence on? Fixing up drugs to sell out here on the streets instead of doing something more productive like going to college and making history by inventing something that would benefit the world. What the fuck is wrong with you?" Mo said through gritted teeth.

T Ski looked at his brother and smiled. "I'm doing this to make money so that I can pay for college and everything else. I need to help out around here. I need to help Mommy. I know what I'm doing. All I need is a little more time to finish this up and get it out there. Trust me, brother, you will be proud of what I come up with. I just need you to trust me. I would never endanger my family or jeopardize our freedom. What I am creating will be in drug stores soon. Trust me, Bro, I've been talking to a lot of people," T Ski assured.

"How is this going to help Mommy? She refuses to go to the doctor. Money isn't the problem solver in her case." Mo retorted.

"Mo, I just need you to believe that everything I have been working on will benefit her and make me a profit as well. I told you, I know many people and I have been doing this for some time now. I just need for someone to sample this so I can see what the effects would be and how long the high would last for." T Ski explained.

"What the fuck you need a crackhead for if you just gave the shit to me. Were you using me as your fucking test dummy? T Ski, I need for you to start making some sense of the shit you have going on in here." Mo was growing angrier by the second. T Ski kept a slight grin on his face. He knew that Mo was not going to allow it if he didn't explain to him what his intentions were.

"I am 100% sure that everything I'm doing here will benefit our whole family. If you want our mother to be on this earth just a little longer, I need you to just hold me down and let me do what you know now that I am capable of doing. I got this, Bro, and if you just give me a chance to show you my operation, you will be just as excited about this as I am." T-Ski grew serious as he spoke.

Mo saw his brother's confidence and couldn't remain angry. T Ski sounded as if he knew what he was doing and had everything under control. "Okay. If you got this, then I am riding with you on it. Whatever you need me to take out of here to give someone, I will. No one is to come to our home for any reason." Mo's phone vibrated. He pulled his phone out of his pocket and saw a message with the answers he needed. "Keep an eye on Mommy for me, please. I have to go handle something," Mo said, heading for the door.

T-Ski nodded in agreement, and then said, "I need to go take care of a few things myself." He was relieved that Mo was going to give him the benefit of the doubt. T-Ski knew things would work out just the way he needed them now that he had his older brother on board.

Chapter 2
Marcus Garvey Projects
Sugar Foot

"How the fuck did you motherfuckers manage to miss this nigga? I swear if you want shit done correct, you have to do it yourself! And what the fuck happen to Brick?" Sugar Foot shouted.

"The nigga shot him," Olli stated nervously.

"If you niggas were chasing the motherfucker, how the hell did he shoot Brick? There were five of you and only one of him. I'm trying to understand this shit, right now."

Sugar Foot heard his phone ring. He looked down at his phone and pressed the button. "Speak on it," He said. He listened intently to what the caller had to say while making faces at his workers. "I'm on it. Good looking. One." Sugar Foot disconnected the call.

The guys stood in the living room a few feet away from where Sugar Foot sat. The room was medium size with just a small TV, a couch, and love seat inside. Krista sat on the window ledge smacking on her gum, noticing how petrified the guys all seemed.

"I want to know where to find someone by the name of Tadow. He's pushing work hard body out here and he needs to be handled. We will deal with this other situation later. Get out there and bring this motherfucker to me." At Sugar Foot's order, the guys hurried out of the room and straight out of the apartment, grateful to still have their lives. Sugar Foot turned his attention toward one of his pops.

"What's wrong? Why are you looking at me like that?" Krista asked as she licked her lips. She already knew the answer to her question. Sugar Foot had spent top dollars to keep a woman like Krista on his arms. She was fine with a nice shaped body. She was of Hawaiian descendant and had a tan color complexion. She was 5 foot 11 inches tall with long jet-black hair that flowed down her back.

Sugar Foot knew that he wasn't a good looking man, but his swag and 10 inch penis made up for the looks. He was the same height as Krista weighing about 240 lbs of fat. He was dark skinned with a low fade.

"Get over here and suck daddy's dick. I need a release." Sugar Foot said, as he leaned back on the couch and unbuttoned his shorts. He pulled his tank top that he was wearing over his stomach then pulled his dick out and massaged it, as Krista took her time sashaying making her way across the room. Krista reached Sugar Foot and dropped to her knees. She took the gum she was chewing out of her mouth and held it in her hand. She moved in closer and moved his hand out of the way. She wrapped her hands around his rock, solid dick and started rubbing it, slowly picking up speed. She knew how Sugar Foot liked it. Krista put her mouth on the tip of his dick and licked around it. Sugar Foot moaned. Krista deep throated Sugar Foot dick taking the whole thing into her mouth. She positioned herself so that she wouldn't get a cramp in her neck. She massaged his balls, as she sucked his dick.

"Damn, girl! You sucking the shit out of this dick. Make me cum all in your mouth." Sugar Foot said, holding his head back enjoying the feeling. Sugar Foot grabbed Krista by her hair and pushed her head up and down on his dick. Entangled his hand in her ponytail, he fucked her face. Krista was use to this treatment. Sugar Foot was her bread and butter. She would have allowed him to piss on her if he wanted to. Krista was busying herself giving Sugar Foot head. When she felt Sugar Foot was about to release, she starting playing with his balls, so that he would hurry up and bust his nut.

"Stupid motherfucker." Sugar Foot had reached his nut, although he heard a voice. He was too busy concentrating on that nut to open his eyes to see who was now in the room with them. Once he had let his entire nut explode into Krista's mouth, he opened his eyes. He couldn't believe what he had saw but before he could say anything, Mo let off two shots in his skull, killing him instantly.

Krista got up off her knees and looked back at Mo. She placed her gum back in her mouth, hurried to Sugar Foot's safe and entered the combination. Inside, there was a duffle bag, already filled with a quarter of a million dollars. She grabbed it and closed the safe door. Krista followed Mo out of the apartment. Once they were outside, Krista tossed the duffle bag into the back of a rental car, hopped in, and speed off. She was getting the hell out of Brooklyn and didn't plan on returning.

Mo walked in the opposite direction. He was now heading over to Van Dyke Projects to see Bella and to drop off the gun. Mo pulled his hat down lower over his face, picked up his pace and hurried. He knew that someone in the next apartment had probably heard the two shots and would be calling police by now.

Van Dyke Projects

Bella was sitting on her couch, watching television when she heard the door unlock. She picked up her .45 caliber from beside her leg and pointed the gun towards the door. When she saw Mo's face, she put the gun back down and turned her attention back toward the television. Bella had started keeping the gun within reach when Mo moved out. Living in this neighborhood, in the roughest part of

Brooklyn, her piece was her security and gave her a little peace of mind.

Mo walked straight to the back of the two-bedroom apartment and put his gun in Bella's closet. He grabbed a shirt that he had hanging on the doorknob and exchanged it for the sweatshirt he was wearing. He then took his hat off and tossed it in closet onto the shelf, closing the door behind him. Mo went back and sat beside Bella. She had moved her gun by now, placing it under one of the throw pillows.

"Why are you sweating like that? You had to know that it was almost 80 degrees outside." Bella asked, as she glanced over at Mo.

"I just put in work. I was sweating with that damn sweater and hat on." Mo replied.

"Who?" Bella asked, as she turned her attention to Mo. It had been a long time since he had killed or so much as hurt anyone.

"Sugar Foot." Mo said.

Bella turned back toward the television. "How is Mommy doing?"

"She's the same. What are you doing tonight?"

"Why?" Bella kept her eyes glued to the television.

"I need you to come to Mommy's crib later on."

"What's going on?" Bella knew that Mo didn't allow people in the house, ever since his mother became ill. She had knew that something was seriously going on or about to happen. Mo took a seat beside Bella. He missed his little family but knew that his mother needed him the most. He believed whole-heartedly that Bella would always be there for him as he was for her.

Bella had been riding out with Mo for 6 years. She was 26 years old and albino. She was petite with small breast, a small waistline, and a wide ass. She was pretty in the face, had blue eyes and freckles with deep dimples. Her blonde colored hair was long and thick, stopping just an inch from her waist. Bella had three brothers and one older sister who now lived on the other side of the country, in California. Bella parents still lived in Brooklyn but had no dealings with her.

Bella was a bad ass, always stayed in trouble. The day that she raised her hand to strike back at her mother, her father put her out the house. She was 14 years old. Bella had a cold heart. She didn't give a fuck about life, at all. She was teased growing up, bullied by peers who'd made fun of her complexion and outdated clothes. Her parents couldn't afford to buy Bella and her siblings everything they wanted but did give them what they needed.

Bella dropped out of school and had been homeless for 5 years, living from house to house with different men she would meet on the street. Once they were tired of her and felt they no longer had use for her, they would put her out. Still, Bella was a hustler. She learned how to survive on the mean streets of Brooklyn through the grace of God. She would run into bathrooms in fast food restaurants to wash her ass and would steal, boost from stores to make sure that she had clothing. When Bella would see her parents, they would just walk by her like they didn't know who she was. Her siblings were no better. They were too scared to even speak because of their parents. It wasn't until her siblings became older that they started helping her out. Giving Bella their allowance and sneaking her into the house when their parents were working, allowed their sister to take showers, eat, change and borrow clothing.

Bella never wanted to be caught in her parent's house. She had rushed out of their home one day when they were on their way back. That was the day she had run into Mo. She was running so fast that she almost knocked him down.

"Damn, watch where you're going, Shorty," Mo said.

"My bad, nigga. You act like I meant to run into you. I was trying to be up out my parent's place before they got home," Bella said, walking away.

Mo started checking his pockets. "Are you a thief or some shit?"

"Why the fuck would you ask me some shit like that for?" Bella asked defensively.

"You running like you stole something," he replied.

"Damn, nigga! I said I was sorry for bumping into you." Bella started walking again. She was trying to catch her breath. She walked over to Marcus Garvey Projects and sat down in front of the bus stop, while Mo watched. He then walked on to Born's house. Born was one of his homeboys. Inside of his apartment, there was a game of spades going on. Mo sat at the window and watched Bella's every move from inside. He wanted to see if she was waiting for someone. He could see the girl was unusually beautiful, but she had a bad attitude and seemed to be up to no good.

Three hours had passed. Mo had since joined his friends in a game of poker and forgotten about Bella until after he'd left the apartment. Stepping out of the building, he looked across the street and saw Bella still seated at the bus shelter, still seated in the same spot. That's when Mo walked across the street and approached her.

"What the fuck do you want now? I don't have any money, dude, if that's what you want."

Mo frowned at her. "I don't want your fucking money. I wanted to know why you still at this damn bus stop, and it's almost one o'clock in the fucking morning. Do you know what goes on around here?" Mo said.

"I was born and raised here. Of course I know. I don't have anywhere else to go," Bella said.

"How old are you?"

"I'll be 20 years old tomorrow."

Mo took a seat beside her on the bench. "Your parents kicked you out today?"

"Why you asking so many personal questions? You don't know me and I don't know you. Unless you got a place for me to crash, I suggest you leave me the fuck alone," Bella said, rolling her eyes.

"You already told me some of your business, so you might as well keep sharing. I might be able to help you out," Mo said.

"I'm not about to be no fucking hoe for a place to stay." Bella stated with attitude while rolling her eyes.

"I don't get down like that, Ma. My mother raised me better. I'm just trying to help you, because I don't think you should be sitting out here this late with no place to go," Mo said.

He seemed genuinely concerned. Bella looked in his eyes and could see the sincerity. Bella then took a deep breath and explained, "My father beats up everybody in the house. My mom use to beat the shit out of me when my father would whip her ass. One day, I just got tired of the shit and started fighting back. She hit me one time with a broom, because I wouldn't give my little brother my juice. I snapped. I jumped on her and beat the shit out of her. My father came home, beat up on me and threw my ass into the street. That was almost 6 years ago."

"Where the hell have you been staying all this time and how were you able to survive with no money?" Mo asked.

"I do what I have to do. I'm good." Bella said. She was dealing with it the best she could. It was what it was. She didn't want pity.

"Come with me." Mo said, as he stood up.

"I'm not going anywhere with you. Like I said, I don't know you." Bella said, turning away.

"Get your ass up and come with me. I'm not about to stay out here all night with you. I have to get up for school in the morning." Bella looked at Mo. He was fine as hell, but she didn't trust anyone. Her instincts told her to get up and follow him. And she did.

A month after living with Mo, it was Bella who had fallen in love. And that's when they became a couple. Bella also decided to go for her GED. Once she had received it, Mo pushed her to go on to college, and she did.

Right after graduating, Bella had become pregnant with their now 5-year-old son Xavier. Xavier was very smart for his age and the cutest little boy anyone could ever lay eyes on. His complexion was very light, and because of his thick curly tresses that hung to his waist, he was always mistaken for Puerto Rican. Mo wouldn't hear of Bella cutting his hair.

Mo, Bella, and Xavier had been living in their own place until Evelyn had fallen ill. When Mo told Bella that his mother was sick, he told her that he had to move back home. Bella thought that he was going to end their relationship, but to her surprise, Mo found an apartment for them in the projects right across the street from his mother's building.

"I'll tell you what's going on as soon as you get there." Mo said. He looked at his watch then stood up to go back home.

"I'll be there as soon as I finish up here. Xavier will be with Tina until I get back." Bella said, standing up from the couch to walk Mo to the door. Mo turned to her and kissed her passionately on the lips, then walked out, closing the door behind him.

Bella was livid. She shook her head as she plopped down on the couch. It had been almost a week since she had seen Mo. And now, he showed up just to change his clothes and drop off a gun with a body on it? This wasn't how she pictured life being with him. They were inseparable from the time they'd become a couple, and now, all that was changing. Bella didn't like it. Mo was also neglecting

37

his duties as a father to their son. She felt like a side chick. She missed how things use to be before moving back to Brownsville.

Bella had compassion for his mother when she first heard the news of the illness. Evelyn was a beautiful and kindhearted woman. When it reached a point where Bella and Xavier started being neglected, that's when Bella began to lose patience. Mo could've been there for them, as well as for his mother. But half the time, he would be too tired to make it back.

Bella headed to the bathroom to shower. She didn't know why Mo wanted her to come to the house later on. But if this would give her an opportunity to talk to him about their relationship, and spend some time with him, then she was all for it. Xavier was down for his nap. She would wake him once she was dressed and ready to take him over to Tina's house.

Chapter 3

Tilden Projects

Mo walked into the apartment. Taz B was sitting in the living room on the couch, watching TV.

"What's up?" Mo said, as he locked the door behind him and walked in, taking a seat beside Taz B.

"Nothing. Shit it's hot out there! Someone got killed in their crib in Marcus Garvey, and cops are sniffin' niggas out, questioning everybody." Taz B said.

Mo didn't respond to that, but knew it was time to get some questions answered. "Why the fuck were those dudes chasing you? Are you out here slinging?"

Taz B cut his eyes in Mo's direction. He didn't fear his brother, but he respected him and wouldn't dare go up against Mo, knowing he would get his ass whooped. "What the fuck do you think, Mo? All I do is go to work and come the hell home to see about Ma. Shit! That was about the most entertaining shit that has happened to me in the last few fucking months. And you know I'm not stupid enough to bring heat back to the crib, here with Ma! Those niggas fuck with me for no damn reason. I don't have beef that I know of. But with these niggas out here in The Ville, they can have beef with you…

just because, without you even knowing why you're their target. You know this."

Mo looked at his younger brother and said, "I just wanted to hear it from you. I went up to T Ski's school today. Niggas say the boy is a genius."

"What do you mean?"

"Just what I said. Our braniac baby brother is an actual genius. I'm going to holla at you, as soon as Bella gets here. How is Mommy doing?" Mo asked.

"She's asleep. I just checked on her about a half hour ago," Taz B explained.

Mo got up from the couch and headed back toward his mother's bedroom. He pushed the door open. They never closed the door all the way. He walked over to her bed and sat down on the chair. He stared at his mother. Although her room was dark, there was a light from the street that shined on his mother's face. She was beautiful. Every time the thought of losing his mother crept into Mo's mind, he would break down. He couldn't help it. He loved his mother more than life itself. He wasn't ready for her to go. Mo stood to leave. He found himself about to get emotional, and he knew that Bella was on her way over soon. It would be hard for him to stop crying, once he started. He didn't want to explain to Bella why his eyes were red.

Mo kissed his mother softly on the cheek and started for the door. "Mo." Mo spun around quickly when he heard his mother's voice. She hadn't spoken since the day she confined herself to her bed.

"Ma, did you say something." Mo asked as he rushed back over and sat back down in the chair.

"Yes." Evelyn opened her eyes and looked at her son. Mo was nervous. This was the first time he had heard her speak in months.

"Are you alright?" Mo didn't know what else to say at the moment because he was still in shock. He tried to prepare himself to hear what she had to say. He prayed that it wouldn't be bad news because he didn't know how he would handle it.

"Tell my baby that I said he has my blessing. God is watching over you boys and anyone else that will be attached to you all. Do what you have to do. I'll be waiting. Protect your family at any cost." Evelyn said with a soft whisper. She then closed her eyes. Mo hadn't the slightest clue what she was talking about. He wanted to ask her but didn't, seeing her close her eyes.

Mo walked out of the room and headed straight for the living room.

"Did Mommy talk to you today?" Mo asked Taz B.

"No. Did she talk to you?" Taz B said with an attitude. He didn't know why Mo would ask him a stupid question like that knowing their mother hadn't said a word in a long while. She mostly nodded when someone spoke to her. The only sounds Taz heard from his mother mouth was when she coughed.

"Yes." Taz B raised a brow and twisted his lips, as if he didn't believe him. Mo walked to the back of the apartment and knocked on T Ski's door. T Ski unlocked his door and stuck his head out. When he saw that it was Mo, he let him in locking the door behind him.

"Did you talk to Mommy today?" Mo asked.

"Yes. I told her my plans and was hoping that she would give me her blessings and respond back, but she didn't," T Ski said with disappointment in his voice. He didn't dare tell Mo that he had given her something to take while he spoke briefly with her.

"I just went in the room to check on her and she told me to let you know that she gives you her blessing. I didn't know who she was talking about at first until you just told me you had spoken with her. She said that she isn't going anywhere and that she will be waiting," Mo replied.

T Ski smiled. He figured that the contents he had given her earlier had taken some kind of effect on her. This was his goal he had and he knew that soon, his mother would be out of bed in no time. "I made a few phone calls. My plans are all set up. I have to be somewhere in the morning. You will need to call Aunt Sheryl here to keep watch over Mommy until I get home," T Ski said.

Mo looked around his room. He looked at his brother with pride, pulled him close to him, and hugged him. "I love you, Bro," Mo said before unlocking the door and walking back to the living room.

Taz B was fast asleep on the couch with a book in his hand. Mo walked over and took the book out of his hand and looked at it. Taz B was reading a book called Silent Cries by Sonovia Alexander. Taz B loved reading especially series about powerful families. The family in the book reminded him so much of his father and uncles.

Mo looked at the back of the book and read the contents. He wasn't too big on reading hood books himself, but the cover caught his attention. There were all kinds of books on their bookshelf in the living room that their sister Andrea had left behind. She loved reading. Mo walked over to the bookshelf and placed the book back. He returned and shook Taz B awake.

Taz B opened his eyes. "Damn, I dosed off. What you wanted to holla at me about? I'm about to head to bed. I'm tired as shit, and I have to be up for work in the morning." Taz B said as he stood.

"Just hold on until Bella gets here. There's some serious shit I need to talk to you two about. Once we talk, then you can go to bed," Mo said, as he took a seat on the couch.

Van Dyke Projects

"Xavier, come put on your shoes. Mommy has to go out for a few, and I'm going to take you to Tina's house, so you can play with Anton until I come back to get you." Bella said, as she fixed her makeup.

"Mommy! Why do I have to go off to Tina's house? I already played with Anton today. I want to stay home and watch my movies that Uncle T Ski bought me."

"Why do you always have to give me a hard time when I ask you to do something, little boy? Get your shoes on and hurry up. I don't think you want me to tell your father that you aren't listening to me." The way her child mind operated, he was too smart for his own good. She couldn't believe what came out of her 5 year old's mouth next.

"Mommy, Daddy doesn't care. I don't even see him anymore. He's always busy taking care of his mom." Bella quickly turned her head. She knew that it was time for her to talk to Mo about their kid. Mo would plan to take him somewhere but would have to cancel at the last minute, because something would come up involving his mother. She was grown and could handle her feelings but it bothered her that now, even her son was feeling neglected.

"Xavier, why would you say something like that? You don't know what you're talking about. I told you about your mouth little boy. You know if your father heard you say that he would be on your behind. Cut it out and stop being so grown," Bella said to her son.

"I'm just telling you the truth. Uncle T Ski spends more time with me than Daddy does. He buys me books and toys. Daddy doesn't even know! And I can read grown up books. He doesn't know that I can take my toy train apart and put it all back together all by myself. Uncle T Ski said that I'm a boy genius like he is." Bella stared at her son, not knowing what to say in response to him. She had seen him fixing things in the house but never paid attention to it. The bedroom door had come off the hinges a few days ago and she had called Mo to come and fix it. Xavier had gone into the toolbox that Mo had in the closet, got out the screwdriver, and was trying to fix the door. She thought it was because he was always watching things like that on television. Xavier wasn't an average 5 year old. He would rather watch the Discovery Channel instead of cartoons. He watched the news and liked "reading" the newspaper. Bella had noticed those things before; but never gave them too much thought until now.

She knew that T Ski was a very bright kid and she loved that he always took time out to come and check on his nephew. He would sit in with Xavier for hours at times, while Bella would go out and run errands. She loved the bond her son shared with both uncles and even his aunt.

"Xavier, please do what I ask and get your shoes on. I have to be somewhere, and I need to go take care of it *now*," Bella said.

"Can I stay home alone? I know how to watch myself," Xavier said.

Bella grabbed him by the hand and led him into his bedroom. "Put your shoes on now, boy! And I'm not going to say it again. You are *not* staying home by yourself. You think I want someone calling ACS on me? Now get your stuff and let's go!"

Hearing Bella raise her voice, Xavier knew now that she was getting upset. He quickly grabbed his sneakers and put them on his feet. He didn't want his mother to put him on a punishment.

Bella didn't like to yell at her son, but she knew that he was stubborn and pig headed just like she was. She didn't want to keep Mo waiting. But she also understood what her son was saying and was definitely going to bring it to Mo's attention in hopes that he would make the time for his family.

Bella and Xavier headed out of the apartment and started toward the elevator. Bella touched the small of her back to make sure her gun was secured. She never left home without her piece. Being with Mo, she knew that he had many enemies even though he was no longer in the streets. Brownsville wasn't the safest neighborhood to live in as well and she felt safe walking the streets strapped.

"Yo, let me holla at you for a minute." Dogg said as he approached Bella and Xavier. Xavier looked at his mother wondering who the guy was.

"Get the fuck out of here, nigga! What the fuck I tell you about that shit? You must hate your life to be showing up at my crib." Bella placed her hand on her .45 while pushing Xavier behind her with her free hand. "I have shit to do, and I got my seed with me. Fall the fuck back, nigga."

"It's not that fucking serious, Ma. I just needed to holla at you about some serious shit. I don't mean no harm. You know we have unfinished business and you don't like answering my calls all of a sudden." Dogg had a smirk on his face. He always did love a chick that was about that life.

"If I don't answer my phone, it means that I'm fucking busy. Get your ass out of my fucking hallway, Dogg! Real talk." Bella couldn't believe the balls this nigga had. He had better considered himself lucky that Mo wasn't around, or he would've found a bullet in his head real quick. Dogg smiled, backing away toward the staircase.

Bella grabbed Xavier's hand and stepped onto the elevator. Pressing the floor above hers, her heart was racing. She prayed that she didn't have to do anything crazy in front of her son. Bella kept that part of her life away from Xavier and wanted to keep it that way.

"Who was that guy, Mommy. What did he want?" Xavier asked. He didn't seem to be scared in the least.

"He was nobody you need to worry about baby. Don't mention this to Tina either." Bella took her phone out of her pocket and sent Mo a text, asking him to meet her half way. She didn't know if Dogg would be waiting outside and she wasn't going to take any chances.

Chapter 4
May 15, 2005

T Ski sat down at the table, waiting for his father to be brought down to see him. It had been a year since he had come here. He hated seeing his father on lock down, like an animal. T Ski looked around the small, space room and saw inmates, some crying, some laughing, with their loved ones. This made him very uncomfortable. He had never come to see his father alone. He was always with his mother. Being that Evelyn no longer left the house, T Ski settled on writing him, periodically, instead of taking the long trip alone. T Ski knew that he had to speak to his father face to face. He had shared just bits of information with his father here and there, telling him of his plans but not explaining in full detail, knowing prison letters were read before given to inmates.

Po came walking through the door. The officer that was escorting him inside the visiting area removed his handcuffs. Po hadn't had a visit in so long, it was shocking when he was alerted. Po soon sat at the table and set his eyes on his son. This was a pleasant surprise but also unusual that his 15-year-old was visiting, without someone over the age of 18.

"T Ski baby, what's poppin'?" Po said, excited. T

Ski stood and hugged his father. Po kissed him on the forehead and then sat back across from him.

"How are you, Pop?" T Ski asked.

"I'm hanging in there, son," Po said looking around for Evelyn. "What's good with you? Where is your mother?"

"I came alone. I need to talk to you, Pop."

Po looked at his son and heard the change in his voice. He knew it had to be serious if his youngest was here alone. "Talk to me son. Is your mother okay?"

T Ski didn't know how his father was going to react, but he had to tell him everything. "No. Mom is sick, Pop. She was diagnosed with some ill shit 6 months ago. Now, she done gave up. She don't go for treatment, take her meds or anything. And she isn't trying to. We don't force her to, either. That's why nobody's been here to see you. Pop, now I need you to listen to me. I'm working on something and I'm going to need some names and numbers for fam, those ride or dies that you introduced me to back when I was younger. And I need you to trust me and not ask any questions. This is serious."

Po looked at his son still shocked at what was just shared. Hearing the news about his wife, part of him wanted to just break down. He assumed that she had moved on and found someone else to love her. He would've preferred to hear that than news that she might be dying. "What's this about, Terence?"

T Ski saw his father's mind drifting. Po was the one who had given them their nicknames. He only called them by their given names when he was upset. "Pop, I just need you to do this for me. Within a year, we will all be millionaires, if not before then. And I will have you out of here. I just need you to trust me. I have to go pop. . I will be home by 3pm. I'm going to need that information from you today. I will be waiting for your phone call. There aren't too many details I can offer up in here. When you call me today, I tell you what I can. Don't use the payphone. Be sure to go to the head and ask for a phone. I got it covered already. I love you, Pop." T Ski stood from the table, walked over, and kissed his father on the forehead. Po remained speechless until he saw his son disappear behind the doors. Po looked around to see if anyone was looking at him. After gathering his thoughts he took a deep breath, stood, and walked over to the guard to be placed back in handcuffs and led back to his cell. He looked at the wall clock and saw that it was 10:40 am. Now he was anxious to know what the hell was going on. Po just had to be patient and wait until 3pm to learn exactly what his son was up to.

McMillan Foundation Center

Once he left the prison, T Ski went down to the McMillan Foundation Center, an office in Midtown Manhattan, for a 12:30 pm meeting. T Ski walked up to the front desk. The receptionist was busy on a personal call. He checked his watch. T Ski didn't want to interrupt the secretary call so after signing his name, he took a seat, hoping that he would not be late for his scheduled appointment. He took his backpack off and placed it on the floor beside his feet and waited patiently.

Once the woman was done with her call, she looked down at the clipboard and up at T Ski's name. Then, she picked up the receiver to their intercom system. "Terence Moore is here. Should I send him back? Okay." The woman now hung up and smiled at T Ski. "Mr. Moore, you can come around, and go through this door to the first room on your left. Mr. Roman is waiting for you."

T Ski grabbed his bag and followed the directions she had just given him. He reached the room and knocked before entering.

"Come in." A deep voice said from behind the closed door.

T Ski walked inside. Mr. Roman was standing behind his desk but came around to greet T Ski. "It's nice to meet you, Mr. Moore.

Please have a seat." Mr. Roman said. T Ski took a seat. Mr. Roman sat back at his desk, opened a drawer, and pulled out a folder.

His office was well furnished. While Mr. Roman looked through the folder, T Ski saw his expensive looking watch and noticed the time. It had just turned 12:30. He hoped that this wouldn't take too long. He wanted to be home in time for his father's call, but this was something that was necessary to put his plan in motion.

Mr. Roman noticed his impatience. "Mr. Moore, I'm sure you know why we called you down here?"

T Ski nodded his head.

"Great. I'm going to go over just the minor details, so you can get going. Is there an adult here with you?" He asked.

"With all due respect sir, I'm capable of handling my own affairs. I have an accountant and a lawyer. Both could be here within 10 minutes time, if need be."

Mr. Roman smiled at T Ski and continued. "Here at the McMillan Center, we offer an award called *The Genius Award*, an honorarium of $500,000, as you know. We received your portfolio a few months back and have sent your samples to the lab for testing. We feel your research may have a positive impact. It has already gained the approval of the review board and that is the reason for your presence here today. We now are awarding you this grant to further your research. And our state's Governor Pataki wishes to meet with you a week from today. Your endowment has been processed. I will just need you to sign here, and let me be the first to say congratulations," Mr. Roman said.

T Ski signed the paperwork. Mr. Roman handed him the check and escorted him out of the building. Once outside, T Ski jumped in the cab that had been waiting out front. He directed the driver while sending text messages, arrived at his next destination in 10 minutes, and jumped out. The driver remained out front.

T Ski walked in a building, headed straight to an office on the ground floor and knocked.

"Come in," Regina said in a cheerful voice. When T Ski opened the door and walked inside, she looked at him and said, "Hello, sweetie."

"Hey, Aunt Regina. I need you to deposit this into the account quick. I'll call you later with further details," T Ski said, passing her the check.

"Okay." Regina opened up a new screen on her computer. She typed in something then grabbed her phone and took a picture of both sides of the check. She uploaded the check and waited. When she saw it appear on the screen, she turned the monitor around for T

Ski to see. Then, she gave him back the check and closed the window.

"Thanks, Aunt Regina. You know what to do, and it all goes down today. I hope you're ready, because you know I need everyone on point."

She smiled at T Ski. Regina knew that her nephew, to be so young, was already powerful. It was crazy that T Ski was going to be bigger than anyone she ever knew of at his age, the age of 15. Watching him grow as a young boy, she always knew he was special.

"I got this nephew," Regina replied.

T Ski left out of the office, thinking about his own nephew. He took a moment and sent a text to Xavier's phone, telling him that he loved him and would be to see him in a few days.

T Ski loved Xavier and knew that he was "different" just like he was. His brother, Mo, didn't have the slightest clue that he had a genius for a son. Xavier was very intelligent and T Ski noticed that when the boy was just a 1-year-old. He had never seen a child that could actually hold conversation at that age. He had bought Xavier children's books and would take them over to Bella's house and have Xavier point out objects on the page that he would name. T Ski didn't share any of this with anyone else, because he had a plan that started from there. A minute later, Xavier text him back, stating that they needed to talk. Bella and Mo didn't know that Xavier now had a phone. It was their own little uncle-nephew secret.

Chapter 5

Tilden Projects

Mo was in the kitchen, making lunch for Evelyn and his Aunt Sheryl, when he heard a knock at the door. He walked over to the door and looked through the peephole. He couldn't believe who was standing on the other side. He unlocked the door and opened it wide.

"Mo!" Andrea shouted as she jumped into her big brother's arms.

Mo hugged his sister. He was glad to see her but thought to himself. *This is bad timing.* "What are you doing here Andrea?" Mo asked, as he broke free from their hug.

"I didn't know I needed a reason to come home. I quit my job, because it was becoming a strain on me, and I'm out of school. I decided to come home and visit my family. Where is everyone?" Andrea said, as she walked into the house with her bags in hand. Mo took the bags from her and sat them down on the living room floor.

"T Ski had to go out, and Taz B is at work." Mo replied. He took a good look at his little sister, wondering where time had gone. She was no longer that young innocent little girl anymore. There was a beautiful woman standing before him.

"Where is mom? Is she at work?" Andrea asked.

Mo grabbed his sister by the hand and led her over to the couch. "I need to talk to you," he said.

Andrea's smile turned into a frown. She didn't like the tone he was using and knew something was wrong. "What's going on, Mo?"

Mo shook his head, not knowing how he was going to explain their mother's condition. He knew that Andrea was very emotional and his mother didn't need to see that.

"I need to talk to you about Mommy, but I don't want you to get loud. She's in her bedroom with Aunt Sheryl. Mommy is…dying, Andrea. We found out about 6 months ago. She doesn't want to go to chemo or take her medication. What she has, there is no cure for it," Mo continued to explain. "She is making it day by day. But without her getting the proper treatment, we don't know how long she will have."

"You guys knew about this for 6 months and didn't bother to call and tell me. How the hell do you think that makes me feel, Mo? What if God forbid she didn't make it through the night? Y'all were going to let me stay away, without sharing what could possibly be the last few days my mother would have left on this earth? That's fucked up and you know it! I'm not a kid anymore, Mo! I have seen and been through just about as much crazy shit as you have! What made you think that I wouldn't be able to handle it?"

"That wasn't why we didn't tell you. I didn't want you leaving school to come back home to look after her. This is why Taz B and I moved back home. You know Mommy wanted us to get our education. I know with you being home, you would feel obligated to sit here with her, and I can't have that. We all made a vow to both Mommy and Pop that we would finish college…no matter what," Mo said.

"There are colleges here, Mo! I love school and would still get my degree!"

"I don't want you attending school here in NY. I don't want to worry about you dealing with these dickheads out here. You know these motherfuckers out here hate us because of who Pop was and what he stood for. I won't allow anyone out here to hurt or disrespect you, Andrea. You already know this!"

"Mo, don't you know that there are niggas everywhere you go? I was brought up right and can take care of myself. You can't protect me from heartbreak. And you can't protect me while I'm all the way in another state. Don't give me excuses as to why I shouldn't be here with my mother!" Andrea now had teary eyes.

Mo threw his hands up in the air, and screamed angrily, "Why didn't you call before you came here?"

"Because every time I call, you guys always rush me off the phone! That's the reason why you guys never let me speak to Mommy! This is some bullshit! I can't believe you, Mo. I am her only daughter. Why shouldn't I be here with her?" Tears had fallen from her eyes, Andrea replied while wiping them away.

"How long are you going to be here?" Mo asked, without acknowledging her feelings or questions.

"I was planning on being here until July," Andrea said.

"When you go in to see her, she probably won't speak. She hasn't talked for the last few months. She doesn't get out of bed, we have to spoon feed her. We take turns looking after her. We give her baths and all. I just thought I'd warn you, before you go in to see her. Don't break down in front of her, please. We don't want her to get upset," Mo said.

Andrea buried her face into her lap and began to weep. She couldn't believe what she was hearing. She was afraid to go and see her mother, not knowing what she was going to look like. And now, she was even more disgusted with her brothers for not telling her sooner.

Mo rubbed her back. "Try to pull yourself together before you go in there to see her," he said.

Andrea wiped her tears away. She stood up from the couch and walked to the bathroom, grabbed a washcloth off the towel rack, and washed her face. When she came out, Mo was standing there. Together, they walked to Evelyn's bedroom. The door was slightly ajar. Mo pushed it open wide and Andrea walked into the room. Evelyn was sitting up in her bed. Sheryl had freshened her dreads with new twists and had given her a bed bath. Evelyn was now smiling, as her sister, Sheryl, was holding a conversation with her about the family.

"Hi, Aunt Sheryl," Andrea said.

Sheryl stood up from the chair and walked over to give her niece a hug. "Hello sweetheart. It's been a long time since I saw you. You look beautiful."

"Thanks." Andrea released herself from her aunt's embrace. "Hey, Mom!"

Evelyn looked at her daughter and smiled. She was happy to see her but was too weak to speak. After the information T Ski laid on her, it had taken Evelyn hours to come up with the words to respond to Mo.

Andrea walked over to her mother's bedside and kissed her on the forehead. Her mother looked the same as the day she had left for school. She couldn't tell that her mother was sick. Andrea had seen people with cancer and saw the end-result after chemo, they didn't look good, at all. Her mother looked well. "I missed you mom. I'm home from school for my break. I'll be here with you until the end of July. Mo already made it clear that I can't stay." Andrea looked over at her brother.

Mo didn't blink and gave her an eye that said with words, you're taking your ass back to school.

Andrea began to ease beside her mother on the bed, Sheryl stopped her. "There is a chair right here that you can sit on. You have just come from outside and I don't want you to sit on the bed with your street clothes on," Sheryl said.

"Okay. I'm going to go take a shower and change my clothes. I want to lie beside my mother," Andrea replied.

Sheryl walked over to the dresser and took out a white gown. She passed it to Andrea. "Put this on when you're done," she said, handing the gown to Andrea.

Andrea took it, looked back over to her mother, and noticed that everything on her mother's bed was white. Even the gown that she had on was white. Andrea understood why.

"I'll be right back Mommy." Andrea excused herself, as she went to shower.

"I'm going to head back. I have to get ready for church. I'll be back next week. I love you sis," Sheryl said with a kiss.

"Thanks, Aunt Sheryl," Mo replied, as he kissed his aunt on the cheek. Sheryl smiled and headed out. Mo walked behind her to lock the door. T Ski entered the apartment as Sheryl was leaving out.

"Hey, Aunt Sheryl," T Ski said, as he kissed her on the cheek.

"Hey, handsome! I was on my way out. I'll see you guys later," Sheryl said, as she pulled the door behind her.

"Are you going to tell me where you were?" Mo asked his little brother.

"I had to go take care of some things. I'm waiting on Pop to call me. I made it home just in time. Try not to hold up the line. I need to talk to him about something very important," T Ski said, as he started walking toward his room.

"Your sister is home," Mo said.

T Ski stopped in his tracks and walked back to Mo. "Where is she?" he asked.

"She's taking a shower." Mo replied.

"Did you tell her about Mommy?"

"Yes. Andrea's okay."

"Good. I'll be right out. Once I get off the phone with Pop, then we can talk," T Ski said, walking away, without waiting for a response.

Mo had to admit to himself that it felt strange to be taking orders from his little brother, but the ball was now in T Ski's court.

Chapter 6

Riverdale Projects

"My nigga, I'm telling you that Sugar Foot is dead! Niggas ran up in his crib and got at him," Lee said.

"That's what that nigga get. That fool was stunting like he was built like that. Fuck that nigga!" Tadow replied.

"Shana is throwing a party tonight in Glenmore Projects. We need to shoot over there. It be mad fiends over there and I'm trying to knock this work off, so I can re-up," Lee said.

"Hold on a sec." Tadow's phone was ringing. He grabbed it and answered. "What's up cuz?" Tadow said into the phone.

"I need to come by your spot and wrap with you. Are you home?" Mo asked.

"Yeah. What's good?" Tadow asked.

"Not over the phone, my nigga." Mo replied.

"I got you. I'll be here." Tadow said.

"Make sure you clear your house. I have business to discuss, and this is for family ears only," Mo shot back.

"It's just me and Lee here." Tadow responded.

"A-ight. I'll be there soon." Mo disconnected the call.

Tadow and Lee were sons of Sheryl. Tadow was 30. Lee was 24. Tadow was dark and stood 6 foot 2 inches tall. He had a muscular body, dark brown eyes and kept his cornrows long, down his back and freshly braided. He sported that look with a goatee and stayed fly. Tadow sold drugs, earning 10,000 a week, easily. Because he worked for himself, he had beef with people from different projects. He had never been to jail, because his game was tight. Lee was rated a pretty boy in the hood. He spent more time tricking on girls and had two kids by different women living in the same projects. Still, he took care of his responsibilities and his women. Standing 6 foot tall even and weighing 220lbs, he had the look of a personal trainer, a muscular body, caramel complexion, and was bowlegged. Lee may have been respectful to women but to niggas, he was straight crazy. Ruthless, he possessed an I-don't-give-a-fuck-about-anyone attitude. If the dude wasn't family, Lee just didn't give a fuck. Still, those times Lee had been to jail were always only on dumb shit dealing with a woman.

These two could almost pass for fraternal twins. The brothers were always together, handling business. They partied together, sold drugs together, had each other's back, and would ride or die for each other. Their father was a police commissioner but wasn't aware of the lifestyle his sons were living. Their father, Perry, lived in Queens with their grandmother, an 87 year-old that had her leg amputated. In that situation, years back, it was Sheryl who decided that it was best for Perry to move from their household and help his sister care for their mother.

"Who was that on the phone?" Lee asked.

"That was Mo. He's about to swing through in a minute. I guess we can wait until tonight and fly by the party and see what's up." Tadow replied.

Tilden Projects
3pm

The phone ring. Mo reached beside him and answered it.

"Hello," Mo said.

"What's up son?" Po replied.

"What's going on Pop?" Mo said.

"I'm good. Where is your brother? I need to chat with him for a minute." Po responded.

"I know. He's been waiting on your call. Hold on a minute." Mo got up from the couch and headed back to T Ski's room. He knocked on the door. "Pop is on the phone." Mo said.

"I got it," T Ski replied, as he picked up the phone in his room. "What's going on pop?"

"You tell me."

"Did you get the information that I asked you for?"

Po took a deep breath and asked his son. "What do you need this information for?"

"I have something planned, and I need my strongest family to have my back on this, Pop. I know what I'm doing. I been working on this for the last 6 months, and I know it will work. I'm trying to make us enough money to get out of New York…for good. And I'm working on getting you out, too. But I need for you to keep your cool while you're in there. Trust me, Pop. I'm a gold mine. You will hear some things about it sooner or later, but know that we will handle things here."

Once again, Po was speechless. He would've never thought he'd hear his youngest son talking like this. It still upset him that his bad temper had fucked up his life and he was unable to be there, raising his kids with his wife. He always knew that they would be good, because he had always instilled in Mo to make sure that the family is good. If anything was to ever happen to him, he knew Mo would handle it. "I believe you son. You were able to pull this off, so there is no telling what else you can do. I got you...in whatever you need," Po assured him.

"Give me the names and the numbers," T Ski said.

Po then read off all the names and numbers to his son. Afterwards, T Ski said his goodbyes and hung up the phone. He took all the information down and pulled up a new screen on his computer and started punching in the names and phone numbers that his father had given him. He knew who each man was and had entered their names in a system that he had already created, which tapped into the police department's server. The first thing he wanted to make sure was that they all had clean records. Next, he went into another screen and checked out their medical history. He didn't need anyone getting sick behind what he had in mind. Once T Ski was done with making corrections to things he saw that needed to be handled, he got up from his computer, shutting it down and headed into the living room where Mo was.

Mo turned his head when he saw T Ski enter the living room. T Ski took a seat beside Mo.

"Brownsville is a cluster of projects. For what I have planned, we need the backing of strong willed people. I will be the brains behind everything and everything that I say needs to be executed exactly, in order for things to run smooth. This is the reason why I only wanted family involved. The first projects we need to move in on are Van Dyke Projects, Brownsville Housing, Langston Hughes Projects, and Howard Projects. The others will come afterwards. Here, on this paper, is a list of names and instructions. Before you move, wait for a phone call," T Ski said, as he stood up from the couch.

"I'm about to head over to Tadow's crib. I'm going to chop it up with him and Lee, and I'll wait for that phone call. Do you want me to pick up Taz B?" Mo asked.

"No. I have something else for him to do. When you get over there, call me, and let me know if they are in agreement. When you answer that call, no one is to hear what's being said to you. Not even those two. Take the call outside, because Tadow and Lee are hot." Mo nodded his head, understanding what his brother was saying. Mo folded the paper up and put it inside of his pocket. He grabbed the keys from the table and headed out of the house. T Ski locked the door behind him and headed to his mother's room.

T Ski pushed the door open and saw her and his sister, both lying in bed fast asleep. They looked beautiful and peaceful. Everything that T Ski had planned would benefit everyone he loved. He loved his mother and was going to do whatever he could to keep her here on earth for as long as he could. He closed the door leaving it cracked a bit and headed into his room. He heard a noise before he could close his door. He stepped back into the hallway and looked around and saw his sister walking out of his mother's bedroom.

"I thought I heard someone walk in Mommy's room, so I got up to see who it was." Andrea said, as she walked toward T Ski. T Ski closed his door and stood in front of it. "Why'd you close your door like that? Do you have a girl inside your room or something?"

"No. I have a lot of things going on right now and it's personal. No offense to you, sis," T Ski replied.

"I want to talk to you about something. Do you know why Mo is trying to get me to go back to school so quickly? He acts as if he's not happy that I'm home. I have been gone for a minute and just wanted to come home and be with my family," Andrea said, leaning up against the wall across from where T Ski stood.

"We have a lot of things going on sis and I'm trying to build something where we will all be set for life. He doesn't want you to get caught up in the bullshit. Things will probably get hot around here in Brooklyn," T Ski explained.

"What do you mean? What are you guys up to? I hope you all don't bring any drama here, knowing Mommy is sick."

"Why would I do that Andrea? I'm trying to make us all rich. I have some things that I have been working on for years, and I know that it will work out. As long as everyone plays their part, we will be good."

"Is this legal?" Andrea questioned.

T Ski looked away from his sister, because he hated liars and lying. He knew that she wouldn't understand what he was trying to do. Instead of answering her, he said, "Why don't you go back in the room and get some sleep?"

"You are classified as a genius. Mo and Taz both have college degrees. I know you three are not trying to go out there to sell drugs for quick cash. Why would you want to mess up your life like that? Mo has a son. I know he don't want his son to grow up without a father like we had to." Angry, Andrea now folded her arms across her chest.

"The less you know the better off you will be. We got this, sis. Don't worry about us. There is no room for mistakes and no one will get locked up," T Ski said, trying to sound convincing.

"How can you be for certain?" Andrea replied.

"I know what I'm talking about, Andrea. Trust me when I tell you that I thought this out to a tee. We will be good. When it's time for you to go back to school, please leave," T Ski said.

"What is wrong with you guys? Haven't y'all learned from Pop's mistakes. Being a drug lord will get you locked up or dead.

I'm sure, because Pop never needed to get his hands dirty, he probably thought he was untouchable. Where did it get him, T Ski? Hard time. Is this what you guys want to waste your life on? I never understood why any young black man would go so hard to sell drugs and poison their own people…just for a quick buck. I thought you all were smarter. I don't know what the hell I came home to…but I don't like it. Our mother is on her deathbed, and you fools are out here selling drugs, instead of doing something positive with your damn lives! What makes you any different than any of these other niggas out here in Brooklyn? Is this the kind of dude you guys want me to bring home?" Andrea looked her brother up and down and then shouted, "I'm talking to you and you're just standing there with no answers!"

"You don't have the slightest clue about what you're talking about. I'm not our father and I'm far from any of these niggas out here. Like I said, what I have going on will get us out of here and help us live better. Everything you're saying to me right now is irrelevant. I don't want to hear all that. I have the blessing of the *one person* I need it from. So if anything, that's *all* that matters to me right now. I'm out to make things happen and I'm going to do just that. And I will die trying, because nothing will stop me. Nothing, at all, will stop me from getting what I need to get. When it's time for you to go, you need to be out." T Ski's words carried an authoritative tone, as he walked away from his sister into his room. He closed his door behind him and locked it.

Andrea slid down the wall and started to cry. She didn't understand what had happened to her brothers from the time she left home. They had changed drastically and she couldn't take it. Andrea loved her brothers to death and didn't want to see anything happen to any one of them. Her return home was turning a surprise into a nightmare, and she didn't know how to stop it.

Chapter 7

Howard Projects
The Beginning...

Rant had just gotten out of the shower. After fucking his baby's mother, he had to hurry up and get her out of the house, before his woman came back. Rant was a 28-year-old hustler. He came from a long line of hustlers and had easily adapted the lifestyle. It was Rant who had Howard Projects on lock down. He had four workers that brought in a total of 15,000 dollars a week. Rant made sure that he stayed on top of them and that his workers never came up short.

Rant was 5 foot 11 inches tall. A high-yellow pretty boy with a smooth baby face. That, and the deep waves he sported, made him look younger than he actually was.

"Kelly, why are you still sitting there? Didn't I tell you I have somewhere to be?" Rant was already pulling his pants up his legs.

Kelly sat on the bed not moving giving Rant the evil eye. "You ain't say nothin' about having somewhere to be, before you brought me up here to fuck me. I'm tired and need to get some rest. You wore my ass out." Rant smiled at the compliment but knew that he still had to get Kelly out the house before Regina got home. He was horny as hell and almost couldn't resist letting his baby mother stay awhile, just to chill out for a minute longer. But Regina was on her way home from work, and he knew if she came in and found his baby mother in her house, he would have hell to pay.

"Kelly, I need to get going. I would leave your ass here but I don't know what time I'm coming back. I'll be by your crib later on, and we can chill for the rest of the night." Rant lied. Kelly sucked her teeth, knowing he was lying. She started getting dress.

"I'm done with this shit. I'm good for you to fuck me when you want, but not good enough for you to be with. I'm the one with your seed, nigga, and don't you ever forget that. You treating me like I'm some straight up hoe! And you know it's not like that, at all. Fuck you, Rant," Kelly said, as tears fell from her eyes. She felt stupid once again and had no one to blame but herself.

Kelly grabbed her bag, once she was completely dressed and started for the door. Rant stood in the room, waiting to hear the door close. He didn't know what to say and didn't want an argument to prolong her stay. He gave it a minute or two, before walking out of the room. That's when he ran dead smack into Regina. If looks could kill.

"I know you didn't just fuck this bitch in my crib, Rant?" Regina said, dropping her purse to the floor where she stood. Ready to beat his ass, she started taking off her shoes.

"What the fuck are you talking about?" Rant said. Nonchalant, he walked into the kitchen.

"Don't fucking play with me, nigga," Regina said. "I just saw this bitch Kelly walking out of my damn apartment, looking like she was crying. She usually talks shit when I see her, but she didn't say one word. That means only one thing. You fucked the bitch and tried to get her ass out of the house before I got home!"

"You're over exaggerating as always. I didn't fuck Kelly. She came to get money for our seed, and I didn't give it to her. She got mad and cursed me out and left." Rant said as he opened a bottle of water he had just taken out of the fridge.

"I'm so sick of you, Rant. You think I'm stupid. You don't know how to be faithful, and I'm getting sick of this shit. You will not continue to play me for a fool. And why the fucks aren't you at work?" Regina asked placing her hand on her hip. She had begged her uncle to give him a job to keep him out of trouble. Her uncle had called her, asking if Rant was still in the hospital. He hadn't come in to work for almost a month. Regina was mad that her uncle had waited a whole month to call her, but then hurried home because now she knew Rant was up to something. He was going to get what was coming to him.

"I wasn't feeling too good today," Rant lied.

"I don't know why your dumb ass keeps lying to me like this. My uncle called me, stupid! He already told me that you hadn't been to work in a month. How the fuck can you be dumb enough to lie to my uncle, like he wasn't going to call me? You know what, Rant? Since you love the streets that much, it's time for you to get your shit and go. I can't help you, because you don't want help. You love fast money, and fast money is only going to get you killed or put in jail for a long time. You had a great life here. At least that's what I thought. If you would rather be in the streets, hustling and looking over your shoulders, than keep a real job, so be it. Get your ass out of my house. I pray nothing bad happens to you. But if something does, I hope you can survive it." Regina picked up her bag and her shoes from off the floor and headed for her bedroom. She was tired and now, was done with him for good.

Mo

Riverdale Projects

"Rant runs Howard projects? We will have to get to that nigga first. His goons are loyal to him, but he is so caught up in his bitches that he can get got at any moment. That's an emotional ass nigga." Tadow said.

"I'm just waiting on the call. That's going to be taken care of. Once he's out of the way, the call will come through, letting us know where his people are. I hope you two fools are ready, because there is no room for fuck ups, right now," Mo said in a serious tone.

"You know we stay ready, cuz. I'm surprised that we are taking orders from a smart nigga like you. Never thought that you would turn to the streets again, but I respect that shit," Tadow said, securing his gun in the back of his pants.

"Turn your phone off. Don't leave it on vibrate or silent. Turn it completely off." Mo said as he took his ringing phone out of his pocket. He looked at his phone and flipped it open. He pushed the talk button. "Yo," Mo said into the phone.

"The nigga is walking out of his building right now. Walk down the block and watch our backs." The phone went dead after the instructions were sent. Mo looked at his cousins and signaled for them to follow him out.

Mo opened the door to the building's second stairwell and ran down with Tadow and Lee, following close behind. When they exited the building, Mo spotted his uncles, already walking down the block with hoodies on. He saw where they were heading and started walking toward them. Mo didn't want to get too close but wanted to be close enough, just in case they needed him. Now, he whispered,

"They said the nigga just walked out of his building. Keep your eyes open. We don't need any fuck ups, right now."

Lee and Tadow said nothing, but nodded their heads in agreement.

Rabbit picked up his pace, checking his surroundings as he walked just a few feet behind Rant. Rabbit's brother, Josiah, was a few steps behind him. And he looked over to his left and saw his nephews in position, not too far behind.

Meanwhile, Rant's attention was elsewhere. Though he was on his way to his workers to collect money, Rant was on his phone. So busy trying to apologize to his main girl, Regina, that he didn't even realize that he was being followed.

"Regina, listen to me. I didn't fuck her. I don't know why you're tripping out like this. If I wanted to beat, I could've gone to her place to do that. Calm the fuck—" Before Rant could finish his sentence, he was hit in the head with something hard. He dropped his phone and grabbed his head. He felt dizzy, and when he managed to see clearly, he tried to turn around but was hit again. This next blow knocked him off his feet.

Rabbit continuously bashed Rant in the head with the steel pipe that had been tucked inside his pants. Once Rabbit saw that Rant was no longer breathing, he and Josiah took off running. Josiah and

Rabbit were Po's brothers. When they were phoned with a request from some random person who claimed to be "blood" but didn't wish to reveal his name, the two were skeptical until Po told them it was all good. And when they were told exactly how much they would receive for getting their hands dirty, and that sealed the deal.

On the opposite side of the street, Mo, Lee, and Tadow continued past, like they didn't just witness Rant's beat down. Once the guys reached the corner, Mo checked his phone. T Ski had sent him a text message, while they were walking. That message let Mo know that he needed to see him before they made any more moves. From the corner, Mo and his cousins parted ways. He told them he would meet them back at their place later, and then he picked up his pace and hurried home.

Mo cut through another project checking to see how many people were out and about. It was the usual faces that he saw. Children were out playing in the park, old school guys were sitting on the bench, drinking beer. People were in their own world.

Mo was still thinking about what had just happened. He needed to know if his brother was ready to deal with all of this bloodshed that would result from carrying out his orders. He knew that his brother was goal-mind, but he wondered. *Did T Ski really know what he was doing and what he was getting them all into?*

Mo reached their building and walked up the stairs instead of waiting for the elevator. He couldn't wait to get upstairs to see what T Ski wanted to rap about.

Chapter 8

Tilden Projects

Mo walked into the apartment, closing and locking the door behind him. He set his keys on the table that was beside the door. He headed into the living room where Taz B was. Taz B looked up at Mo and then continued reading his book.

"You still reading that damn book?" Mo said as he sat down beside Taz B.

"Yeah. This shit is alright though," Taz B said.

"We need to go meet up with Tadow and Lee in a little while. I texted Bella and she's on her way over here. Shit just went down, and we knocked one nigga off the list. Well, Uncle Rabbit did." Taz B looked at Mo. He thought it was a game when he had gone over the details with him and Bella. He didn't like the idea of taking orders from his baby brother. Taz B didn't want to get knocked for nothing stupid. He wanted to finish this semester, get done with college and get a real job, paying good money.

"Why are we going over there? I don't know if I believe this shit is going to work. What the fuck are we trying to take over the projects for? We good now, money! Just living our lives, low key and legit is fine by me. I'm not tryna get caught up in no bullshit. We have income coming in. What the fuck is T Ski thinking?" Sarcasm was in Taz B's voice.

Mo frowned his face and looked his brother straight in the eye. "Listen, nigga. I don't want to go to jail either or get killed, but this is to help Mommy. The shit that T Ski is doing and the shit that he got going will give us more than enough money. And with that, we can help keep our mother here just a little while longer. Now you can bitch up if you want to but when the money comes, don't try to be getting down. I have a fucking son to take care of and I do want to be around to raise him, but I also want my mother around long enough to see my son grow into a man. Yes, we have jobs. But that's not enough money to get us the fuck out of here! T Ski got a plan that will get Pop out of jail, so he can be home to be with Mommy. I know if Pop tells her that it's time to leave Brooklyn, she will go. We need *all* of our family involved. We're stronger together. That's better than having outsiders betray us and fuck up what we are trying to do. I believe that T Ski knows what he's doing," Mo said through gritted teeth, trying his best not to raise his voice and alarm his sister.

Taz B scratched his head and nodded in agreement. "Alright man. I'm down. But if I feel, in the least bit, that shit ain't going right, I'm out."

Mo didn't even respond. He shook his head, got up from the couch, and headed toward T Ski's room. He knocked on the door. T Ski opened the door, knowing it was Mo on the other side.

Mo walked into the room, took a seat on T Ski's lazy boy chair, and said, "Riverdale projects head is done."

"I know." T Ski locked his door and sat down at his computer. He turned on the monitor and faced the screen to Mo. Mo looked at his brother and didn't know what to say. He was in total shock. T Ski continued, "I saw the whole thing from here. Uncle Rabbit did well and the best thing about it was no one was around to witness anything." He zoomed in on the scene and Mo was able to see the cops and the large crowd of people that had gathered around Rant's body. An ambulance was just arriving and EMS workers were rushing out of the truck.

Mo, watching along with T Ski, now said, "Let me ask you something, Bro? Does it bother you to watch what you are putting into progress? Now that this is done, there is no turning back. Are you going to be able to handle this mission that you're on?" His tone was serious.

T Ski turned to look at Mo. "I know what I'm doing, Bro, and it's going to benefit a lot of folks. What I'm putting out is to help the people, not kill them. These ruthless ass dudes are out here killing their own people for a quick buck. What I have is a drug, but one that won't affect or harm the ones that are looking for a fix. Once we get what is needed, then we're gone. By the time they realize what it was, it will be too late. I just need you to make sure that my identity is kept secret, because I will be dealing with the government soon because of my gift. I told you, all I need is just for you all to knock those dudes out of the box, and we're good. I got these earpieces for you and Bella. I know that Taz is not feeling this whole idea, so I don't think it would be best to put *him* out on the streets, handling business. I have something else in store for him. I sent out a mass text to everyone, and I wrote everything down for you." T Ski then handed Mo a sheet of paper with writing on it. Mo took it and looked it over and listened. "I need all of this done tonight. I will keep watch for you guys and let you know what's going on. Bella needs to be in and out. There is no room to mess up, Bro, so please let her do whatever she has to. I have been watching these dudes for some time and I know their routines. These pieces are for Tadow and Lee. It's a little past 8pm. If you can get to these two spots before 11, then you are good. If you don't get shit done before that time, then I need you to back off." T Ski now turned back to his computer.

Mo looked at him, got up, and walked out of his room. In the living room, he looked over the instruction, reading them over and over, until they stuck in his head. Taz B glanced at his brother but didn't disturb him. He continued with his book.

There was a knock at the door. Mo folded the page and put it in his pocket as he went to answer it. Looking through the peephole, he saw that it was Bella. Mo grabbed his keys and unlocked the door. "Taz, I'll be back soon. Check on Mommy and Andrea before you go to bed."

Taz B nodded. He knew what that meant. He was not invited to do whatever it was that T Ski had just commanded Mo to do.

"Hey, babe. Are you ready?" Bella asked, once Mo was in the hallway.

He locked the door and then reached over and kissed her on the lips. "Yeah. Where is Xavier?"

"He's with my sister. She's going to keep him for the night," Bella said and they both headed for the stairs. She knew her son didn't want to go to his friend's house, so she took him to her sister's instead. He was better off there anyway. Bella knew now wasn't the time to talk to Mo about Xavier. She was planning to speak to him about that before the night was over.

"Here, put this in your ear. Don't ask any questions." Mo remarked. Bella took the earpiece and placed it in her ear. It was so tiny. She hoped she would be able to take it out.

Once they were out of the building, they walked toward Riverdale projects, which was minutes away. Mo took the paper out of his pocket and started going over it again. He read it four more times before he ripped the paper into tiny pieces throwing it in the nearest trash receptacle.

They soon reached Tadow's building and was at his apartment. Mo knocked on the door. A moment later, Lee unlocked and opened the door and led them inside.

"Where is Tadow?" Mo questioned.

"I'm right here," Tadow said, as he came out of the bathroom.

"We—"

Before Mo could get a full sentence out, T Ski voice was heard, "Uncle Rabbit and Josiah are waiting for you guys downstairs. You got a minute to explain to them what's up and make your way downstairs," T Ski said.

Bella looked at Mo, because she also heard him.

"We are going to Van Dyke projects and Brownsville houses tonight. Barry is a nigga that stay low key because the Feds are watching him. Bella is going to do her thing, and we will go in once

I know it's good. From there, we are going to pay Big L a visit. He has two dudes with him at all times. Make sure your shit is loaded, because it's on. Uncle Rabbit and Josiah are downstairs waiting for us so we need to move now," Mo instructed.

The guys and Bella didn't waste any time. They walked out of the apartment and down the stairs without stopping. They reached outside and met up with Rabbit and Josiah. Bella walked ahead of the guys, as Mo filled his uncles in on what they had planned.

"You guys need to split up. Let Uncle Rabbit go with Lee and Tadow and Uncle Josiah go with you and Bella. It would make it easier and quicker," T Ski said into Mo's earpiece.

Mo gave the instructions and told them all the info that they needed. Once they were done handling business, they could call it a night. He was going to have more info tomorrow on what the next move was.

Sonovia Alexander

Chapter 9

Van Dyke Projects

"Who the fuck is it?" Barry shouted from behind his door.

"It's Tina. Is Keisha home?" Bella said. She heard the door unlock. Barry opened the door and let Bella in. Bella was in disguise. She had heavy of makeup concealing her pale face and was wearing a one-piece jumper suit that had long sleeves. The wig Bella wore was long and jet-black. Bella rolled her eyes, as Barry looked her over and licked his lips.

"Keisha went out for a minute, but she will be right back. Do you want to sit here and wait for her?" Barry asked. It had been a month since he'd been laid, and he needed something to get in to. He wasn't about to tell this chick that his girl had broken up with him 3 months ago and no longer lived in his apartment.

"Sure." Bella looked around. It was filthy. All over the floor, there were tall bottles of liquor with cigarette butts inside. And when Bella saw the futon that served as his couch, she felt sick to her stomach. The color looked as if it was once white, but it was covered in filth and stains. Anyone would've believed muddy shoes had walked over the futon. Bella tried to hide her disgust by smiling at Barry.

"Should I just sit anywhere and wait for her to come back from the store?" Bella asked in a seductive tone.

Barry grabbed his pants, holding on to his penis, as he licked his lips and quickly lied, "You can sit wherever you want to sit baby. I been seeing you around and I always wanted to approach you but I just didn't know how to do it."

"Aren't you my girl's man? I don't fuck with men who are already in a relationship," Bella said, as she sat down on the edge of the futon. She had to keep talking to keep from throwing up. She knew that she was here for a reason. She hoped that it wouldn't take too long to find out who else was in the house. She tried to think quickly, because roaming through the filthy apartment, wasn't an option.

"We're not together anymore. She just stays here from time to time. Why don't you come over here and sit on my lap?" Barry said as he sat down on a lazy boy chair across from where Bella sat.

Bella wanted to gag. She was ready to go. Bella thought about her purpose for being there and sighed, as she got up and did as she was told. Barry grabbed her by her waist and sat her on his rock hard dick. He pulled her hair aside and kissed on her neck. Bella moaned to get him open but wanted to vomit. He reeked of musk and stale cigarettes. "You're making me feel so good. Is there anyone else here with us?" Bella asked, as she started to unzip the top of her jumper, but he was really grossing her out. She couldn't allow this man to roam his hands over her body.

"It's just me and you baby. Why don't you let me taste that sweet pussy? If we hurry up before my boys get back, I can give you the best dick you ever had," Barry said, pulling Bella closer to him.

A second later, Mo kicked the door open and ran in following behind Rabbit with their guns drawn. Mo had got the word from T Ski that Barry was alone but told him to be careful just in case he was wrong.

"What the fuck?" Barry screamed pushing Bella to the floor.

Mo walked over to him and hit him in the face with the butt of his gun. He continued to pound Barry in his face, as blood gushed from the side of his head, but Mo didn't stop. Barry began to cough and blood spew from his mouth. Mo continued to bash him across the face, and Barry's eyes were now rolling in the back of his head. Meanwhile, Rabbit was running through the apartment, double-checking to see if anyone else was inside. In less than 3 minutes, Bella, Mo, and Rabbit ran out.

"Once you make it outside, you and Bella need to walk in the opposite direction of Uncle Rabbit," T Ski instructed.

As Mo emerged from the building, he grabbed Bella by the hand. "Go the other way, Uncle Rabbit. I'll hit you in a minute," Mo said, as he and Bella walked off.

T Ski heard a knock at his door. He knew it could only be one of two people but was not in the mood to entertain his sister or brother. "What is it?" T Ski asked, still looking at his computer screen.

"I need to holla at you real quick, Bro," Taz B said.

T Ski typed in a few things on his computer and closed the software program out. He then turned his earpiece on mute, stood, and stepped into the hallway to see what his brother wanted.

"What's up?" T Ski asked.

"Bro, I just wanted to rap with you, real quick. I know Mo thinks that I don't have your back, but I just don't want to get caught up in no bullshit. When I went to college, I started thinking differently and wanted more for myself. I just want you to know that I love my family. I will do whatever needs to be done, as long as it doesn't fuck up what I've been working so hard for," Taz B said.

"I understand and I wouldn't do anything to bring harm to any of us. I have something I *will* need you to do. Help Aunt Regina keep numbers and put some things in order, as instructed. You can give her a call in the morning, and she will tell you what she would need from you. That should make you feel a whole lot better. Now,

I have work to do," T Ski said, then stepped into his room and locked the door behind him. T Ski shook his head and returned to what he had been doing.

Brownsville Houses

"Yo! Why the fuck are you playing, nigga? Roll the fucking dice again and stop cheating, before I bitch slap your ass," Big L said to his friend Tone.

Big L had Brownsville Houses on lock down. Big L, Tone, Slim, and J Hood were standing out front playing C-Lo. This was something that they did every night, while making their money. Big L was 6 foot tall, weighed close to 300 pounds, and this big dude was ruthless. No one was allowed to see anything without his permission. He didn't care about anyone but his money and his women. Big L was born Leonard Reeds. He had lost his mother to a car wreck when he was 9 years old, and he never knew his father. He got his nickname from the uncle who had raised him. Big L had grown up in Brownsville and was known around the hood. He didn't stomp on anyone else's ground, and they dared not to step on his. Big L was pulling in at least $25,000 a week but wasn't flashy. He was about getting his paper and saving up. He also opened a studio to produce his own music, as well as lay down tracks for his two boys, Slim and J Hood. They had grown up next door to him and were like brothers.

Big L's Uncle John was a hard working man. Because his sister only wanted the best for Big L, he did everything he could for his nephew. But Uncle John felt his nephew was lazy and didn't have drive. He even tried getting Big L a job at the site where he worked. Big L had been selling drugs since he was 14 years old; he wasn't going for it. Now, he was 24, still doing the same hustle but working for himself. That was the only difference from when he started out. It was easy getting connected to someone's team as a youngster because every big drug dealer needed a stupid kid, one that wanted to stay fly. It was the stupid kid that handled the dirty work for them.

"I'm about to go take a piss. Hold my money right there," Big L shouted. He walked around the side of the building, where he could take a piss.

Tadow, Lee, and Josiah were already at their posts, watching every move. Josiah pulled out his gun and dug into his pocket for his silencer. But aiming his gun, he couldn't get a clear view of Big L. "Cover me," Josiah said. He then separated from the rest, moving in closer around the back of the building, where he could sneak up. Big L could sense something wasn't right. He looked up and saw

Josiah aiming his gun a few feet from him. Big L quickly reached into his back pocket for his own piece, but was too late. Before he could get to it, Josiah already had a bullet through his head. Big L's corpse dropped.

Josiah retreated, trying to get out of dodge before any of Big L boys found him. Running in the direction he had come from, he shouted, "Move!"

Lee and Tadow then took off running. "Go straight home. You guys are clear. Once you hit the corner, be cool and split up." They heard through their earpieces. Once they had run a distance away, they paused to catch their breath. They all looked at each other, confused. It didn't sound like Mo's voice in the earpiece. Who it was that was looking out for them was puzzling?

Chapter 10

Van Dyke Projects

Bella unlocked her door and walked inside. Mo followed, locking the door behind them. He was tired as hell and couldn't wait to take a shower and get some sleep. He wanted to make sure Bella was good, before he left out to head back to his mother's.

"I need to talk to you about Xavier." Bella said as she walked over and sat down on the couch. She grabbed the remote from off the coffee table and turned on the television. Mo sat beside her on the couch and waited for her to talk.

"What's going on with him?" Mo questioned.

"I had a talk with our son today, and he surprised me. I had asked him to go put on his shoes, so that I could drop him off to hang out with Anton, and he started back talking me. He was talking about how he could stay home and take care of himself. And he said that you didn't care about him, because you're always with your mom. Xavier said that you don't basically know anything about him. I couldn't believe the things coming out of this little boy's mouth. He spoke like he was a grown ass man. The boy is really something special, Mo. He took apart his train and put it back together. He wants you to know that he can read grown up words. He also told me his uncle said that he was a boy genius like him." Bella surfed through the channels looking for something good to watch, as she explained.

When Bella said her last sentence, Mo sat up on the couch. "When did T Ski tell him this?"

"I don't know. You know T Ski is always over here with him. He could've told him that any time. Xavier never said when," Bella replied.

Mo stood. "I need to see my son. I'm going to go pick him up."

"My sister is knocked out. You can come and see Xavier tomorrow. Why are you so anxious to go get him now?" Bella raised a brow.

"I need to know if he's anything like T Ski." Mo responded

"What are you talking about, Mo?"

"T Ski was tested in school and the boy is a genius. He is the brains behind this whole operation. We all knew that the boy was smart but not that damn smart. Now you're telling me that our son said that his uncle told him that they were the same. If Xavier is gifted, then we need to have him tested. My son will have a bright future, and I'm going to make sure of that," Mo said, proudly.

"So…it took for me…to tell you…that Xavier thinks he's a *genius* for you to now want to spend time with your son? I told you all that your son shared, Mo. What about the other things? Why is the part about him *possibly* being a genius standing out more than everything else? Your son said that you don't care about him, because your too busy taking care of your mother. How many promises you made to him have you broken? He needs his father, Mo…and I need my man back. Your sister is home for a while. This is the time that you need to be spending here with your family. We are still your family, right?"

Bella was upset and tired of coming second to his mother. She wanted her man home with her and their child where he belonged. She understood the condition of his mother but how long was she supposed to wait to have her family back together. This arrangement wasn't fair to her or Xavier.

"I care about everything you said, and I heard it all. I will talk to him and let him know why I'm not home like I should be. This is what we are working hard for now. T Ski has a plan that will make us all rich and get us the hell out of Brooklyn like we planned on doing years ago. I'm going to give you everything I promised you, Bella." Mo said in a sincere tone.

"How long do I have to wait for that? I'm tired of sleeping alone. I'm tired of holding our son when he's crying, because once again, you didn't come see him like you said you would. I heard this all before, Mo. Now, I'm tired of *hearing* it; I need to see it. Your son needs you more now than ever and not because of his intelligence. He needs to feel loved by his father. He wants you home with us. I have given you my all and been the best woman I know how to be. How long am I supposed to sit around and wait for all this to happen? I shouldn't have to feel like I'm a single parent. I'm sleeping with fucking guns under my pillows, because I'm alone and afraid. You just left us!" Bella had tears falling from her eyes.

"I didn't leave you, baby. I'm right here. I had to go home and take care of my mother. You knew this. I'm not cheating on you. All the bills are paid, and you and my son are taking care of. I can't turn my back on my mother, because that's not an option. That's not the kind of man I am."

"I know what kind of man you are, Mo, and I didn't ask you to abandon your mother in her time of need. I just asked you to be here for your family more. Why is it that T Ski spends more time with Xavier than you do? Why is it that T Ski knows more about your son then you? You don't see that as a problem. Yes, T Ski is his uncle but he's not you. You have to do better, Mo. I will not allow you to keep hurting our son like this. You can consider this as a warning. I am not going to put my child through what I had to go through as a child. That is *not* going to happen. You need to make time for your family…or where moving on."

Mo frowned his face at Bella. "I know you're not threatening me. I wish the fuck you would ever *think* about taking my son away from me. It would be a cold day in hell for you, and I put that on my life!"

"Your threats don't mean shit to me, motherfucker. You forget that I'm not scared of you or any other motherfucker walking this earth. I'm not about to let you walk all over me, because I'm not a weak bitch. Nigga, I know the struggle all too well, and I'm not afraid to go back to it. You can't take from me what I have built in the last few years. I held you down…the same way you did me. I'm telling you to give your family more time, because we're tired of seeing you only when it's convenient for *you*. Your aunt comes and sits with your mother for the *whole* day. Your brothers are home *all day* when they get inside. Why is it that you still don't make your way over here? Is there someone else occupying your time and keeping you from us? Don't bulk up at me, because I'm speaking the truth! What I said…is what I mean. You will make time for us or we are out!"

Mo stared long and hard at Bella. He loved her because of her boldness, and if he wasn't the man that he was, he would've beaten the shit out of her by now. Mo knew that he had to get out of the house before he said something that he would regret. He knew Bella was speaking the truth. He was just too stubborn to admit it. He wasn't seeing anyone else, but he was so busy worried about his mother that he neglected the other important people in his life. He didn't know how to handle losing the one woman that had always been there for him. Mo felt better when he was home with Evelyn. Just in case she took her last breath, he wanted to be there. Mo reached for the door and looked back at his woman. He hadn't seen Bella cry in all the years they had been together, because he made sure to keep her smiling as often as he could. It hurt him to his heart to learn how his 5-year-old felt. He knew that he was only picking an argument because he didn't want to hear what he knew was the truth. Mo walked out of the apartment, closing the door behind him.

Bella got up and locked the door. She had enough for one day. She headed to the bathroom so that she could shower. She knew that she had struck a nerve. She was glad that he was mad because she was dead serious and meant it. She loved Mo more than anything in this world, but she wasn't going to keep living like this. She deserved better and so did Xavier.

Chapter 11

Tilden Projects
May 16, 2005
Mo

Mo woke up in a cold sweat. He had dreamed about Bella. Because of the argument, he and Bella had the night before; he tossed and turned all night. He felt like crap and knew that he had to make it right between the two of them. Mo got out of bed, put on a t-shirt, and knocked on the bathroom door to see if anyone was inside. When it was clear, Mo took a piss, washed his face, and brushed his teeth. When he was done, he opened his mother's door and saw her sitting up in the chair set aside for visitors. Mo wondered how the hell she had gotten into that chair, forgetting that his sister was still there. "Ma, are you okay? What are you doing out of the bed?" Mo said as he walked over to her.

Evelyn looked at her son and smiled. She was just plain beautiful, and for a moment, he couldn't tell that she was sick. She looked the way she looked before her health had taken a turn. Mo noticed something else different about his mother this morning. He stepped back and looked her over. That's when he noticed her hair was gone.

Mo instantly frowned his face and shouted, "What happened to your hair?"

"I cut it. Her hair was damaged and was thinning out. No one has been taking care of it. I will start from scratch," Andrea said, as she walked into the room holding a food tray in her hand.

"Why would you cut her hair?" Mo's annoyance was obvious.

"Because it needed to be done! I didn't need your permission to do so. She's my mother too," Andrea said, now placing the tray on the end table. She sat down on the bed and picked up the toast. Grabbing her mother's hand, Andrea placed the toast in it.

"Andrea, she doesn't feed herself," Mo said.

"That goes to show you that you don't know everything. She does know how to feed herself. Go ahead and show him, Mama." Andrea said looking at Evelyn. Evelyn smiled and took the toast into her hand and put it up to her mouth. She took a bite of it and chewed it. She then swallowed it while taking another bite of the toast.

Mo stood there in silence. He hadn't seen his mother do anything for herself in months. All he could do was stare. He had no words right now.

"Is Taz B or T Ski up?" Mo whispered.

"Taz B left a half hour ago and T Ski is in the kitchen eating." Andrea said as she handed her mother a glass of juice. Mo left out of the room and went to the kitchen.

"Did you know that Mommy is in the room feeding herself?" Mo asked T Ski.

"Yes. I have been giving her something to take to help her build her strength. It's a slow process, but she will get better," T Ski said, as he continued to eat his breakfast.

"I need to talk to you. I walked Bella back to the apartment yesterday, and she told me some things that Xavier had shared with her." Mo said, as he sat down at the table across from T Ski.

"It's true. I heard everything. You forgot to take off your earpiece. I'm sorry that it came out like that, and yes, it's true. Xavier is a genius. I knew it since he was one years old. I didn't share with anyone, because I didn't want anyone to know about me, as of yet. Your son loves you, Bro, and don't think no different. Bella loves you, as well. She cried all night long. You need to go and be with her and your son. I got things here under control. I have some people out in Van Dyke and Brownsville houses moving K2O. I will see how the people react to it and if it will sell. Cops are on a hunt, but they have no possible leads and neither do Big L's boys. No one has reported Barry's body yet. Now, it's just a matter of waiting to see what happens. If all goes well, everything will run smooth," T Ski shared.

Mo was about to respond to what his brother said when he heard a knock at the door. Mo looked at T Ski with a questioning look. He wondered if he had someone coming to the house to meet him. T Ski shook his head, as if to say he didn't know who it could be.

Mo stood from the table and walked to the door. He looked through the peephole and saw his son standing on the other side of the door. Mo unlocked the door and swung it open pulling his son inside and looking around the hallway.

"How did you get here, Xavier?" Mo asked his son.

"I walked here. My aunt dropped me home and couldn't take me upstairs because she had to go to work. I knocked on the door and Mommy didn't answer. I came over here, because I didn't know where else to go." Mo looked at his son and picked him up off his feet and held on to him. He hugged his son tight. Xavier wrapped his arms around his father's neck hugging him back. He loved his daddy and was glad to see him. Mo kissed his son on the forehead and put him down. He locked the door and took Xavier by the hand, leading him towards the back room. "Mommy, look who's here."

Evelyn looked over toward the door and saw her grandson. Her eyes lit up. She smiled and stretched out both of her arms for Xavier to come to her.

Xavier released Mo's hand and walked over to his grandmother. He embraced her and held her. Evelyn squeezed her grandson and didn't want to let him go. She had missed him dearly. Xavier pulled from the hug and looked at his grandmother. He wiped away the tear that he saw creeping down her face. "I missed you, Nana. I know that you're sick, and that's why I couldn't come over. I missed you a lot." Xavier said, as he smiled revealing his dimples.

Evelyn's heart melted. Xavier was so handsome. He looked over at his aunt and went to her to give her a hug.

"I missed you so much, nephew. How are you?" Andrea said.

"I'm doing well. I missed you too. Can grandma talk?" He questioned.

"Not right now. She doesn't have much of a voice." Andrea responded. Xavier looked at his grandmother and began to speak in sign languages. Andrea looked back at Mo. She didn't know that he and Bella were teaching Xavier sign language.

"Xavier, you know how to use sign language?" Mo asked.

"Yes. I just told nana that I hope she gets better soon so I can come over all the time." Mo was speechless once again. He needed to go and speak to Bella. It was time for him to pay more attention to his son.

"Xavier, come with me. I'm going to get dressed and we're going to go see where your mom is. I will bring you back to see nana later on today. You can spend the whole day with her okay." Xavier smiled. Mo loved to see his son smile. He knew that he had a lot of lost time to make up for.

Van Dyke Projects

Mo and Xavier had reached the apartment. Mo unlocked the door and walked in with Xavier behind him. Then, he went straight to Bella's room. When he opened the door, he saw that the bedroom was empty. He knew she couldn't have gone anywhere far, knowing that Xavier was coming home today. Mo walked around the room to see if there was any trace of her having been there. Now, a funny feeling in the pit of his gut told him something was wrong. Mo walked out and headed into the living room. He looked around for Bella's purse and spotted it on the floor in the corner. Mo looked around the living room but didn't see anything questionable. Mo entered the kitchen and saw that everything there seemed okay.

"Xavier, where are you?" Mo shouted.

"I'm in my room checking on Mommy." Xavier said. Mo rushed back toward Xavier's room and saw Bella stretched across his floor with blood spilling into her blouse.

"No!" Mo screamed. He ran over to Bella. Pushing his son out of the way, he knelt on the floor beside her. "Call 911, Xavier! Tell them to come quick!" Mo said as tears fell from his eyes. Mo checked Bella's wrist for her pulse but couldn't find one. He grabbed her into his arms. Whoever came into his family home and did this...was dead.

Xavier came running back into the room with the phone in his hand. "They are coming, Daddy. Is my Mommy dead?" Xavier asked.

Mo grabbed a pillow from Xavier's bed and tucked it under Bella's head. He released his hold of Bella and went to his son. Mo picked Xavier up and walked out of the room with him. He didn't want his son to see his mother like that. He knew that it might damage his son. Mo couldn't think of anyone that would do something like this. He had done some things that he wasn't proud of and so had Bella, but she didn't deserve this.

10 minutes later, there was a loud knock at the door. Mo put Xavier down to open it. EMS workers rushed into the apartment toward the back, as Xavier ran over to Mo and wrapped his arms

around his father's leg. Mo reached down and picked his son up again. A second later, there was another knock at the door. Mo opened the door and more EMS workers walked in. Mo pointed to the back. Afraid, Xavier held on to his father for dear life. Mo knew that he couldn't leave and had already called T Ski letting him know what had happened. T Ski told him that he was on his way over. Mo could never admit to anyone how scared he was at this moment. He couldn't bear to lose his girl. Bella was his world and he needed another chance with her to give her everything he promised her. Mo couldn't hear what the workers were saying in the back and wondered what was taking them so long to bring her out. Mo started to walk toward the back. When someone else knocked at the door, he snatched it open.

"Is she alive, Bro? T Ski asked as he rushed into the apartment.

"I didn't feel a pulse when I was back there. I don't know what the fuck happened and who could've done this foul shit. She was shot, man, and when I came here, the door was locked." Mo said, trying to fight back tears. T Ski walked to the back where Bella was. Mo could hear the workers telling T Ski to step back. T Ski shouted a few words down the hall that Mo couldn't make sense of from the living room with the television playing. Mo stood, waiting for T Ski to walk back in, but he didn't.

Mo paced the floors for what seemed like hours, even though it had only been 7 minutes since T Ski had gotten there. Xavier was watching the Discovery Channel, while Mo softly chanted a prayer. He was scared and didn't know what they were doing back there. Mo stopped pacing when he heard footsteps in the hall. EMS workers were walking Bella out on a stretcher an oxygen mask now covered her face. And T Ski was running, alongside. "Mo, I'm going to ride in the ambulance with Bella to the hospital. Meet us at Wyckoff Hospital. We got a pulse, but it's very weak. I will explain more once we get her there."

Mo stood in shock unable to speak. He didn't know what was done in the back room, but he knew that he didn't feel a pulse.

T Ski didn't wait for Mo's response. He followed the EMS workers out of the apartment and out of the building.

"Xavier, come on. I'm going to take you back to the house with your Nana and Aunt Andrea," Mo finally said.

"No, Daddy! I'm going with you! I wanna see Mommy!" Mo knew that his son was going through just as much and, for that reason alone, decided that he would take Xavier with him.

He knew that if anyone deserved to be in this situation was really him, not Bella. She had such a hard life; he just wanted her to enjoy

the best that life has to offer. They had been through so much together. He knew he could always count on her. Mo started to rethink
everything he was doing. Always strong, always the protector, he
realized things were now getting to a point where anything could
happen to any one of them all at any given moment. These conse-
quences were real. Karma was a bitch and Karma would always
come back. Now, Mo couldn't contain his tears any longer.

Chapter 12

Wyckoff Hospital

"Mo, I'm over here," T Ski said, as Mo and Xavier walk into the hospital.

"Where is she? Did she make it or not?" Mo wasn't sure he was ready to hear the answer.

"She's stable. She had caught a bullet to the chest. The doctors are still working on her. I'm not an employee or doctor, so they wouldn't allow me back there. I wish I had a degree or something. I really wanted to be there to assist in any way I can, but I cannot, no matter how much I know. I'm sorry, Bro. They said it had to have happened about an hour ago. Her pulse was weak, but as they were working on her, I was able to sneak her something that did bring her heart beat back to normal. Let's just pray that everything works out for the best," T Ski said.

Mo was still shaken up to understand or appreciate what his brother had tried to do. Right now, his mind was on his woman. All he could think about was Bella. Mo picked his son up and cradled him in his arms. He was supposed to be their protector, but he had failed them. He promised himself, if Bella pulled through this, he would marry her. From this day forth, he would be the man Bella wanted him to be.

T Ski walked over to the nurses' station, giving Mo space and time alone with Xavier.

"Is the chief of staff available?" T Ski asked.

The nurse looked up at the young boy and rolled her eyes. With an attitude, she said, "You wouldn't find the chief of staff sitting around in the Emergency Room. Why don't you go down the hall. On your right, there's a door that has Chief-of-Staff on it. Go knock on that door, and check for yourself."

"Why are you being nasty? If you don't like your job then quit." T Ski said, annoyed before walking away.

T Ski walked toward the area that the nurse had sarcastically indicated. When he looked back and saw a doctor approaching Mo, he rushed back to hear what was being said.

"Thank you," Mo said to the doctor who spoke briefly and walked off. Mo hugged Xavier tight. T Ski approached, wondering what the doctor had said.

"What's going on, Bro?" T Ski asked.

"They were able to stabilize her, but it still don't look good. I'm gonna need to get some money up, so I can make sure she has the best care. Bella doesn't have insurance. She's not under my coverage," Mo said.

"Don't you worry about nothing. The bill will be taking care of. Let me catch up with that doctor. I'll be right back." T Ski jogged off.

"Mommy is going to be okay. The doctors are going to take good care of her," Mo said to his son. He hadn't been able to put Xavier down. Through this trying time, his child was his source of comfort.

Tilden Project

Mo, Xavier, and T Ski had walked up to their building. Ron D was standing outside and had been waiting to see Mo.

"I need to holla at you, Bro," Ron D stated.

Mo looked at his son and then to his brother. "Take him with you, T, and I'll be upstairs in a minute," Mo said. Once T Ski and Xavier were out of earshot, Mo turned to Ron D, "What's the word?"

"There's a hit out on you and your family. What happened to your girl, that was Barry's people. Someone who got beef with your cousins has been watching your whole family. Them niggas ratted you out on Barry's hit and now them niggas is out for blood."

"Good looking, my man. I'll be in touch." Mo said, as he headed into the building. It was now on and poppin'. Now Mo needed to have a talk with T Ski immediately.

Mo walked into the apartment and locked the door behind him. He headed straight back to T Ski's bedroom door and knocked. T Ski opened it and let Mo in.

"There's a hit out on us. Word is out that we were responsible for Barry's hit." After relaying to T Ski everything that Ron D had just told him, Mo spat angrily.

T Ski pulled out his phone and began texting someone.

Seeing this, Mo grew impatient. "What the fuck do you have planned? Because, right about now, I'm ready to kill every last one of these motherfuckers! Including them two stupid mother fucking cousins of ours!" His blood was boiling, and he was ready for war, but knew that he couldn't do it alone. Mo looked around and noticed Xavier wasn't in the room. "Where is my son?"

"He's in the room with Mommy and Andrea. I'm about to set something up. You need to focus on what we're doing, and let me handle the rest. Give me twenty minutes and I'll have good news for you," T Ski said nonchalant.

Mo screwed his face up at his brother. "Yo, this ain't a fucking joke, Ski. Do you know what the fuck is going down? We have hits out…on all of us. It ain't safe to walk these streets no more. And I got my fucking seed here with me now." Mo wasn't sure if he could handle losing his woman, while still dealing with everything that needed to be done for his mom. And now that a hit was out on his family, Mo was an emotional wreck.

T Ski turned on his computer and started typing. Then he pulled a chair out and motioned for Mo to sit. Several of projects in Brownsville were already on the screen. A second later, T Ski received a text. He looked down, read the message, and smiled to himself. "Just sit here and watch," T Ski said.

Mo looked over at the screen and just waited. A second later Mo jumped, startled by noise coming from outside. Shots were ringing off. "What the fuck?" Mo shouted. "Let me go and check and see if Mommy and Xavier are good."

T Ski grabbed Mo and stopped him. "Watch," T Ski said.

Mo looked at the screen and could see men firing shots at each other running down the street. Mo looked closely but didn't know who the men were. He and T Ski watched things play out. A patrol car showed up on the scene, and they watched as two cops hop out of the vehicle, firing at all the men. Mo never saw anything like this before. It looked like a scene from an action movie. Mo couldn't believe that this was happening, only a few projects down from where they were. They watched people ducking for cover. More cops pulled up on the scene and joined in.

"This shit is crazy." Mo said, as he continued to look on.

"When I said I got my family, I *got* my family, and I won't let harm come our way. I mean that shit. I'm the motherfucker that will get shit done. No one in this hood can fuck with me or mine. I got this shit on lock. I hope you believe me now, Big Bro, when I tell you, I got this. Now, I need to get some work done. Why don't you go tend to your son? I have more things I need to get done. We are about to take over, and I hope you're ready for it. Because now, you need money to help your girl out just as much as I need it to help Mommy. We're gonna make the money, and get the hell out of Brooklyn for good. We got 6 months to pull this off. Shit is about to get real. And when all is said and done, niggas are going to know who the fuck *T Ski* is."

Mo looked at T Ski. Everything his brother just said was indeed facts. He didn't know who T Ski had text or how the scene before them was played out so quickly. Mo no longer recognized this kid, the kid who he had raised for the last ten years like he was his own child. Mo wondered. Who was his baby brother becoming and was this someone that he would be able to love? T Ski was making shit happen like he said he would and it scared Mo a bit. Not even he, himself, ever had this much drive. Mo was in total agreement on one thing, when all was said and done, and people would come to find out that it was a 15 year old making all of this shit happen, niggas was definitely going to know who his brother was.

Chapter 13

May 17, 2005

The Marriott

Taz B had just gotten off work. He was exhausted. He had pulled a double and couldn't wait to get home to catch up on some sleep. It was almost 7 am. He had been at the hotel since 6 in the morning the day before. Taz B had gathered his belongings before clocking out from work. The cab he had called was already waiting outside to take him home. He was so tired that if he were to take the Subway, he'd probably fall asleep and miss his stop.

"Mr. Moore. Hold on one minute." Ronald Shepherd said, approaching Taz B. "I need to talk to you about the new trainee. She starts her first shift tonight. Luis will be out. I was hoping that you would be able to come in and train her."

"Mr. Shepherd, I just pulled a double and was hoping to take the night off, so I could catch up on some of my class assignments. I have finals coming up, and I need to start reviewing my notes." Taz B wasn't down for coming back in to cover someone who was probably out partying late and couldn't make it in to work. That was always the reason why his coworker Luis would call out.

"I apologize and I know that you have your studies, but I really do need you to come in and cover for Luis. I can't allow someone else to train her. No one else is as familiar with our procedures."

Taz B wanted to tell him no, but didn't. "I'll be here." Now he hurried to the front entrance so he could get home and get some sleep. That's when his phone started going off. He grabbed his phone from his pocket and answered. "Yo," Taz B said, climbing inside the cab.

"Where you at?" Mo asked.

"I'm leaving work right now, heading home. I'm getting in the cab right now as we speak."

"We have some work to put in tonight. I need you to stay with Mommy."

"I have to come back in to work tonight, and I can't get out of it. I have a new employee that's starting and no one else can train her. Andrea is home and could look after her until you get back home." Taz B heard Mo suck his teeth over the phone and felt like Mo didn't believe him. But he had to work and wasn't about to risk his job when there was no money coming in from the work T Ski was putting out.

"I'll holla at you when you get in." Mo disconnected the call.

Taz B placed his phone back into his pocket. As the driver was in route, he leaned his head back and thought about leaving town. He loved his family but he was tired of living the way that they were. He didn't want to get caught up in the drug game. He had been down that road before and it never turned out good for him. He couldn't understand why they needed to take over Brooklyn when his father had no luck at trying. T Ski was certified as a genius but what did that mean. He wasn't jeopardizing himself, going out there, putting in hard work, not knowing if he was going to walk away without catching a bullet or getting locked up. Taz knew that this was supposed to be a family business, but it wasn't the kind of business he wanted to be a part of.

Taz B paid the driver, as he exited the vehicle. He checked his surroundings before heading inside the building. Ron D was standing inside the lobby and held the door open as Taz approached. He gave Ron D dap and placed his bag on the floor to chat a bit with his friend before going upstairs.

"What's good son? You just getting in from work?" Ron D asked.

"Yeah, son. I had to pull a double shift and gotta be back tonight. I'm tired as fuck." Taz B explained.

"Did you holla at your brother to find out what's going on in the hood?" Ron D pulled a Black n' Mild out of the pack that he held in his hand and sparked it up. He inhaled the smoke, blew it out, and then extended the pack, but Taz refused it.

"Nah, I spoke with him briefly over the phone and was going to holla at him once I got in. Yo, I'm about to head upstairs but I'll check you later. Good looking out that day son. I appreciate you having my back." Taz B said, giving Ron D a pound.

"You already know, fam, how we do over here. Nothing but love this way. I'll holla at you." Ron D exited the building, while Taz B walked over to the elevator that was already open and took it straight to the 4th floor. He wasn't anticipating hearing what Mo had to talk about when he reached the apartment. All he wanted was some sleep. He knew that wasn't going to be an option, already knowing they were all up in the house at this hour of the morning.

Taz B unlocked the door, entering the apartment. Mo was seated at the kitchen table reading the newspaper, while Xavier sat across from him eating a bowl of cereal.

"Good morning," Taz B spoke.

"Good morning, Uncle Taz. Are you just coming in from work?" Xavier asked.

"Yes." Taz B answered, as he sat his book bag in the bottom of the hallway closet.

"I want to go to work with you to see what you do." Xavier shared.

"I'll take you with me. One day, when I go pick up my paycheck, I'll show you around." Taz B sat down next to Xavier and turned his attention to Mo, who kept his head buried in the paper not even acknowledging Taz's presence.

"I can't wait." Xavier said with excitement.

"Do you need to holla at me, before I go get me some rest? I'm dead tired right now and need some sleep," Taz B said.

"Nah. You good, son. Go get you some rest, and I'll talk to you later." Mo said, still not looking in his brother's direction.

Taz B knew that Mo had an attitude but he was in no mood to entertain it this early in the morning. He could barely keep his eyes open.

Taz B stood from the table and walked toward the back of the apartment. He stopped by his mother door and peeped inside. He saw his mother and sister both asleep. Taz B continued, passing T Ski's bedroom door, which was closed. Taz B reached his room and headed straight for his bed, plopped down, and closed his eyes. He didn't bother to undress or to even kick his shoes off. He wanted nothing but sleep.

"Daddy, are we gonna go see Mommy today?" Xavier asked Mo, while washing out his bowl and spoon.

"I would have to call the hospital to make sure that you are allowed to go up and see her," Mo answered.

"They can't keep me from seeing my mommy. I'm her son. I want to be there when she wakes up. She needs to see me." Mo looked at his son. He couldn't believe the conversation they were having. He wondered if it was possible that his son really was a genius. He was already making plans to contact some of the people and places T Ski's principal had told him about. Mo was definitely going to make sure that his son's future was protected.

"Xavier, I understand what you're saying, but things don't work like that. There are other patients in the hospital, and when they're in ICU, sometimes even adults are not allowed inside to see their loved ones," Mo explained.

"Daddy, I know…but I still want to see my mommy. She will feel my presence."

Mo sighed, "Xavier, there are a lot of things I need to take care of since your mother is unable to do it right now. You have to go back to school, and I need to take care of a few other things before

I can even make it up to the hospital. I'm going to see what I can do about getting you up to the hospital to see your mother, before the day is over. Okay?" Mo understood his son was missing his mother and he was going to make sure that he got the okay from the doctors to bring Xavier up to see Bella. There were other things he had to do first, and he couldn't have Xavier as a tag along when handling business.

"Okay. Are you done reading the paper, Daddy? I want to see if they have anything in the paper about Mommy's accident." Mo closed the newspaper and passed it to his son. Xavier took the paper and headed out of the kitchen toward the living room.

Xavier wasn't really concerned about finding an article. He and his uncle had a daily newspaper ritual and this day was no different.

Mo stood from the table and walked toward the living room. He stood there for a moment watching his son go through each page of the paper reading and looking over things. Mo was mad at himself for not paying closer attention to his son. Mo didn't begin to read well until around age 7, but even then, he never cared to read a newspaper like Xavier. Mo had been praying for Bella to pull through. He wanted his family back, but was going to be the best father he could be to his son while Bella was away.

Mo had already told Andrea that he would need her to look after Xavier while he ran errands. He figured after he informed Xavier school of his mother's condition, he would go straight to the hospital to check on Bella and see if it was possible for Xavier to come see his mother.

Riverdale

"Rob! Rob! Get up now! JB was just shot in the park. Get your ass up out of this fucking bed now!" Veronica screamed, trying to contain her tears.

"What the fuck are you talking about now, Veronica?" Rob rolled over out of his sleep. He had been drinking and smoking all night with his boys and had just walked in an hour before.

"Did you hear what I just said to you, Rob? Your brother has been shot." Veronica was getting pissed off. She was on her way to work when she saw the ambulance in front of the building. As she got closer, she saw the workers lifting a man up on the gurney. There were only a handful of people outside, so as she passed through the park and join the crowd, gathered around the parked ambulance, Veronica saw that it was JB, her boyfriend's brother. And she ran straight back to tell a drunken Rob what had just taken place.

Rob's words slurred. "What the fuck?" He was coherent. He heard what Veronica said to him but he couldn't seem to pull himself together. A second later his phone started ringing. Veronica grabbed it from his pants, lying on the floor.

"Hello," Veronica answered.

"Veronica, where is Rob? They shot JB." Theresa managed to say through sobs.

"I know, Theresa! I just saw him. They put him on the gurney. I was on my way to work. I ran back up to wake Rob and he's too damn drunk and high to even respond," Veronica said, crying herself now.

"You have to get him up, Veronica. I'm afraid to go to the hospital alone. I need him to come with me," Theresa replied.

"Give me a few minutes, and I'll call you back. I'm going to get him up right now." Veronica remarked, as she walked toward the bathroom. She ended the call and placed the phone in her pocket. She grabbed the small pail from beside the tub, took the mop out, and placed it beneath the bathtub faucet. She turned on the cold water and let it run. When the pail was half-full, she cut the water off and grabbed it, carrying it back to the bedroom. Veronica then pulled the covers back from Rob's body and tossed the water on him. Rob jumped up out of his sleep.

"What the fuck is wrong with you girl? That shit is cold." Rob shouted.

Veronica wanted to laugh but this wasn't the time. She sat the pail down on the floor. "Get your ass up, nigga. We have to go meet your mother. JB has been shot," Veronica said.

Rob looked at her and knew that she was serious. He grabbed his pants off the floor but felt they were wet. He walked over to the closet and pulled out a fresh pair of sweat pants. He pulled his shirt off and grabbed a clean t-shirt. "When the fuck did this happen?" Rob asked Veronica, as he tied his sneakers.

"I don't know. As I was leaving out, heading to work, I saw EMS putting him on the gurney. I didn't realize it was him until I got close."

"What the fuck is he doing out 7 o'clock in the fucking morning? That nigga don't start school until 8. I'm going to kill a motherfucker if my brother die! He's only 16," Rob said through tears. It had started sinking in that his baby brother had been shot. "Where the fuck is my phone?" Rob now looked around the floor in search of his phone.

"Here. Call your mother. I have to call out of work." Veronica replied passing it to him.

Rob snatched the phone out of Veronica's hand and started off for the door. "Oh shit. Go grab my wallet and my keys out of my pants pocket." Rob snapped.

Veronica sucked her teeth turning on her heels to head back into his room. Rob unlocked the front door to the apartment, and waited so that he and Veronica could walk out together. His head was pounding and he felt weak. He didn't trust shit right now.

"I got it." Veronica yelled, as she came from out of his room. She handed Rob his belongings. Rob placed his wallet in his pocket and held on to his keys. He swung his door open but wasn't prepared for what was about to take place. Rob had come face to face with death.

Rob froze. Veronica didn't realize there was a pistol pointed in his face, until it was too late. The trigger was pulled and Rob caught a bullet in his head and dropped instantly. Veronica's screams were met with final shot. This one in her head. The culprit walked away without remorse, while both Rob and Veronica lay dead, in the comfort of their own home, in a puddle of their own blood.

Chapter 14

Wyckoff Hospital

Mo rode the elevator up. So much was on his mind. It bothered him that the last conversation he and Bella had, he walked out and left her in tears. And now, he even doubted if T Ski's plan would work, since it hadn't protected his woman. Mo was in deep thought until the elevator stopped at Bella's floor.

Mo walked past the nurses' station, holding up his Visitor's Pass on his way to Bella's room, Room 346. He stopped there, noticing the nurse cart outside of the door and waited patiently for the nurse to exit the room.

"Good morning. Who are you here to see?" the nurse asked, seeing him as she was coming out of the room.

"Bella," Mo said flatly.

"There is no one here by the name Bella, sir," the nurse replied in a soft tone.

"I was just here yesterday to see my girl. She was in this room!"

"Would you like to take a look inside, sir? There is no one in this room. We discharged someone yesterday, but I don't believe that was the name of the patient," the nurse said.

Mo looked at her like she had lost her mind. He moved to the doorway. Peaking inside of the room, he saw that it was empty.

"What the fuck is going on? Where is my girl?"" Mo shouted.

The nurse didn't know what to tell him. She had just came on the late shift and was now preparing the room for a patient that was about to be sent up. "I'm sorry sir. I didn't mean to get you upset. If you go over to the nurse's station, one of the nurses may be able to assist you further," the nurse replied.

"I'm sorry. I didn't mean to get loud, Miss. Thank you," Mo said as he turned on his heel heading over to the nurses' station. "Excuse me, I was just told by the nurse that my fiancé isn't in her room. I was just here yesterday and wasn't told that she was going to be moved. Can you tell me where she is?" Mo asked now in a calm tone.

"I remember seeing you here. She was removed from the hospital by her parents. They didn't give any specific reasons why they wanted her moved. I can call the doctor in for you, if you would like to speak with him. But that's all the information I can provide you with at this time."

Mo was confused. Bella hadn't talked to her parents in years and he didn't know how they found out about her being in the hospital when he was her only emergency contact. Mo knew something wasn't right, and he had to find out what was going on before he lost his cool.

"I would like to speak to the doctor then," Mo said. His phone started ringing before the nurse could respond. Mo pulled his phone out of his pocket. He looked at the Caller ID and saw the house number. "Hello," Mo answered.

"Mo, it's me Andrea. You need to get to the house *right now*. There is a lady and man here, trying to take Xavier. They have the police here with them, and they claim to be his grandparents," Andrea said nervously.

"What! They better not touch my fucking son. I'm on my way!" Mo hung up the phone. He ran through the hall to the elevator. Shit was getting to him and he was going to kill somebody if they tried taking his son from him. He didn't give a damn who it was. Xavier was his son, and no one was just going to take him away.

Mo waited for the elevator. He dialed T Ski's number, wondering where the hell he was. That boy knew the rules. There was always supposed to be a man present in the house at all times. Mo was fuming. T Ski wasn't answering his phone. Mo dialed Taz B's number as he stepped inside of the elevator pressing, for the lobby.

Mo couldn't believe this shit was happening right now. He hadn't even been out of the house a good three solid hours yet, and all this crazy shit had taken place. Bella had been moved without his knowledge, her parents were now trying to stake claims on his son, and he couldn't reach either of his brothers. Mo was ready to fuck someone up.

When the elevator reached the ground floor, Mo swiftly headed toward the hospital's exit. He had forgotten about the pass in his hand, until a security guard stopped him and asked for it. Mo handed it to him and kept on moving. He had to hurry home.

Tilden Projects

"His father is on his way here. If you don't have a Court Order, I am not letting you in." Andrea said from the inside the apartment's locked door.

"We just want our grandson!" Rhonda yelled from the other side. They didn't have an order from the court stating that they would allow Xavier to be removed from his home.

"You can take that up with my brother when he gets here." Andrea screamed, now walking away from the door to sit on the couch. She wished Mo would hurry up to the apartment. The police had already left because there was nothing they could do about removing the child without court orders.

Mo reached the floor and saw Bella's parents posted outside the door. He didn't see any police with them.

"How can I help you and how did you find out where I lived?" Mo asked, still breathing heavily from running up the steps.

"I'm Bella's mother. I'm here to get my grandson." Rhonda said.

"I'm not giving you my son! My son doesn't even know you! Where the hell have you been for the last six or seven years. You damn sure haven't done anything for Bella, because I'm the one that has been there for her. Like I said, you're not taking my son anywhere. You can try your luck in court, but I promise…you won't win," Mo said through gritted teeth.

Rhonda adjusted her clothing and looked Mo up and down. The guy looked plain crazy, and she wasn't about to push the issue any further. "I might not be able to get my grandson from you now, but I can control what happens with my daughter. You are not to see her, and I will definitely let it be known at the hospital she's in that I don't want you there. You keep your child, and I'll keep mines," Rhonda stated. She then walked around Mo, over to the elevator with her husband following behind.

Rhonda had more heart than her husband did. He didn't utter a word. He had warned her before they came up to the apartment that if the police didn't stay with them, they shouldn't be there. He didn't know anything about this man or his upbringing. But Roger was aware of how these young dudes were out here in Brownsville. They shot first and asked questions later. His wife usually controlled and handled things better than he did anyway.

"You can't stop me from seeing the mother of my child." Mo shouted over his shoulders while putting his key in the lock and opening the apartment door. Rhonda ignored him as she and Roger waited for the elevator. Mo walked into the apartment locking the door behind him.

"I'm glad you're here. Did you see Bella's parents?" Andrea asked coming from out of the back room.

"Yeah. I don't know how they got my fucking address or why they came here looking for Xavier. He don't know them and never saw them a day in his life. Fuck them old motherfuckers. Where is T Ski?" Mo asked already heading toward the back of the apartment.

"He's not here." Andrea replied. Mo turned around with a confused expression on his face. When he left out this morning, T Ski said that he would be in the house all day. Mo had told him to keep watch over his mother and son.

"Where the hell did he go?" Mo questioned.

"He got a phone call from someone and left out of the house afterwards. He just told me to keep the door lock and watch Xavier and Mommy," Andrea replied.

"Where is Xavier?" Mo asked.

"He's in the room with Mommy asleep. I'm so glad that he was asleep when his grandparents came here. I didn't want him to see anything like that. They were yelling and shit, acting all crazy. The shit was crazy," Andrea said.

"I'm here now. I don't think they will be showing back up here." Mo put his keys down and walked into the living room, sitting down on the couch. He grabbed the remote control and turned on the television. He had to find out where the hell Bella was moved too. All he needed was for her to wake up and not see him around. She'd start thinking that he abandoned her. He had a lot of making up to do to her. Mo didn't care one bit what Bella crazy ass mother had to say. No one was going to keep him from seeing his woman.

***

An hour had gone by when Taz B walked through the door. Mo was asleep on the couch. Taz B went straight to the back to check on his mother and sister. He opened his mother room door and saw Andrea and Xavier, lying beside his mother watching television. Taz B waved as he closed the door behind him. He headed back into the living room and sat down on the couch. He had just gotten in from doing a run for T Ski. He was pissed that these motherfuckers didn't care that he had been working all day and all last night up until this morning. He needed his rest. He had only been asleep a good 2 hours, before T Ski woke him up to take some product to some of his workers.

"You just getting in?" Mo asked as he opened his eyes.

"Yeah," Taz B said with an attitude. T Ski had sent Mo a text letting him know that he would be sending Taz out to take some of his people work since he was handling business concerning Xavier.

"What the fuck is your problem?" Mo asked as he sat up on the couch.

"I'm done with this whole shit! I don't want any parts to it! T Ski don't know what the fuck he's doing, and I'm not going to be missing out on sleep to be helping run drugs over to niggas through-out the projects. When he told me he wanted me to keep the books and other shit, I was down. But now, he got me running shit all over the place. I'm not with it," Taz B replied.

Mo just looked at his brother. He wanted to reach over and slap the shit out of him for acting like a bitch.

"Yo, stop acting like a fucking pussy. We are doing this for the money to keep Mommy alive and now Bella," Mo said, as he stood from the couch.

"I don't believe that shit! How much money do he really need? And how do we know the shit he mixed up won't do more harm than good for Mommy? I don't know why you're letting him gamble with Mommy's life. Like I said before, I don't want no parts of this shit anymore. I'm done. I haven't fucked in a week, because I'm running around the fucking streets. I'm going to work late and falling asleep. Then they got me working double shifts and shit. I'm not getting no real fucking sleep. I don't see *no money* coming in from all this shit T Ski got out in the projects. And I'm not trying to lose my fucking job," Taz B said, kicking off his sneakers. Mo wasn't in the mood for his brother's shit. Mo grabbed his phone out of his pocket and called T Ski to find out where he was.

Brownsville Houses

"Yo, my name is Rock. I been seeing y'all niggas out here for a minute now. I heard that 'ol boy got knocked off. I use to move product for him. I'm trying to get put on. I hear that y'all got some powerful shit moving out here now," Rock said.

Sonovia Alexander

Joey looked Rock up and down, sizing him up and turned his head away. He could see that Rock was weak. He wasn't about to put no weak ass niggas on his team. He had come from Jersey all the way here to lock this project down with his people. He didn't know who the person was that contacted him but couldn't't refuse the deal.10,000 dollars up front. Joey was a down ass nigga and was all about his paper. He was told that he would only have to be out here for 6 months. This wasn't too far from home for Joey.

Joey was Spanish and just turned 22. He had never met his mother or father. He grew up in the system, and being that he never had anyone to give him the love as a child, as an adult he didn't know how to give it to anyone in return. When Joey had turned 14, he had left a group home after he stabbed one of the residents there. He was tired of niggas jumping him, because he was a pretty boy.

Joey had just come in from school one day. Tired from playing basketball, he dropped his bag on the floor as soon, as he entered the room he shared with three others. He stretched out on his bed hoping to fall asleep. His roommate, the one they called John John, tripped over Joey's bag, while entering the room. John John picked the bag up from the floor and slammed the heavy bag into Joey's back. Joey jumped up from the bed. His back was hurting from what he thought was a punch. Then, he saw his book bag lying on the bed and John

144

John standing there laughing. Joey rubbed the lower part of his back. He had all his books inside and wondered why this dude would come in and just start picking with him.

"What the fuck you do that for?" Joey said in anger.

"Nigga, stop leaving your shit on the floor! I almost bust my ass tripping over that shit. Next time I'm going to just fuck you up. You better be lucky I have somewhere to be." John John stated as he walked over to his bed. Joey snuck up behind John John who was one of the dudes who had jumped him just the week before. Joey had tucked away a pocketknife he'd found on the ground in the school yard. He grabbed that pocketknife from out of his sock, and before John John could turn, Joey stuck the knife in his back.

"Ahhhh!" John John screamed out in pain. He tried to grab whatever it was protruding from out him but couldn't reach it. John John looked at Joey who was now laughing. He couldn't believe this dude just stabbed him and was sitting their laughing instead of trying to get help. John John managed to run out of the room for help. Joey knew he would probably go to jail but didn't care. He would've bet money, though, that that nigga would think twice before fucking with someone else in that home.

***

"Nah, we good son." Joey responded.

"I'm saying my nigga, I'm trying to eat too. Shit is hot right now, and I'm just trying to keep some bread in my pocket," Rock explained. Rock was getting mad. He didn't like having to ask a nigga to let him eat where he was from. Rock saw how dude sized him up and he wasn't feeling that at all. Although Rock was 6 foot tall and weighed 200lbs, Joey met that weight and some. Rock knew that if he tried some shit, he wouldn't get far, because they were at least 10 deep.

"Didn't he say we were good?" Beans said with attitude who was Joey's right hand man.

"Aight son, you got that," Rock said as he walked off. Rock knew that he was going to see those niggas again.

"Yo, what time you got?" Joey asked Beans.

"It's almost 3. What's good?" Beans questioned.

"Round these niggas up and tell them to tally that shit. It's time to make moves," Joey replied. They had been out there since midnight and Joey needed to get some rest. They would be right back out there tonight and every night, until they moved all the weight that was given to them.

"I got you." Beans said as he pulled out his phone. He sent out a text message to all the workers they had been moving K2O in Brownsville Houses. When Joey came to Brooklyn, he brought 24 men with him. The caller needed nothing but ruthless niggas and needed numbers.

Of course Joey was skeptical about the call but once he heard who the dude was connected to, he quickly agreed. This was a come up for him and his team, and he wasn't going to pass up the deal. There would be someone to pick up all the money that was made at 4 pm every day at the hotel they were staying in. They each had to bring a side bitch with them, so it wouldn't make shit hot for them. No hotel was going to let almost 25 men rent rooms for a week without calling the police, thinking that they were up to no good. They would be staying in different hotels each week never staying in the same location for too long.

Joey and each of his men were given earpieces and were informed where police were located, and when to move out. Joey never been involved with shit like this and knew that whoever the nigga was that they were working for had to be one powerful nigga to know every move the boys and his workers made. Joey had already warned his boys that if they crossed this nigga, they would probably be killed. Everyone was grown and came, knowing the risk. Any man caught, slipping or doing some shit they weren't supposed to be doing, was on their own.

Joey had made it to the hotel where he was staying in. When he entered the room, one of his groupies Erica was sitting on the bed butt naked watching porn. Joey wondered if he was interrupting something. "Hey baby. I was waiting for you. I know you told me you would be back around 4. I was making sure that this pussy was ready for you." Erica said as she spread her legs wide, so Joey could take a look at her fat, neatly shaved pussy.

Joey pulled off his t-shirt and threw it across the room onto the chair that sat in the corner. "I need you to count this money over for me first then we can get down to business." He watched Erica's ass jiggle, as she walked over to the dresser, pulling the money machine out of the drawer.

She grabbed the bag from the floor and placed it on the chair. Then she removed the cash, stacking the bundles on the machine to be counted.

A half hour had passed when she finished counting the money. She wrote the numbers on a piece of paper and taped it on the outside of the bag. She then placed all the money back inside the bag neatly, handing the bag back to Joey. Joey took the bag and left the room. He walked into the hallway, headed 3 rooms down, and knocked. There, he sat the bag in front of the door and walked away. Joey was not trying to get caught slipping at any given time. He didn't come here to get killed or locked up. He came to handle business and to keep collecting his dough. By the time Joey reached his room, the door had opened and all Joey saw was a hand reach out and grab the bag. Joey closed his door behind him, and reentered his room. He looked over at the clock. He could only get one good nut off and try to let Erica get hers off before he'd fall asleep. He was tired as shit and needed to make sure he got some rest.

Sonovia Alexander

Chapter 15

Tilden Projects

T Ski had received the call from Mo, but didn't answer. T Ski figured whatever Mo needed to talk to him about couldn't have been important and just had to wait until he made it back home. He didn't need to be distracted while he was out. Mo was seated in the kitchen, staring out the window, when T Ski entered the apartment.

"Do you know where Bella is?" Mo questioned without looking up at T Ski.

T Ski admitted, "Yes, Bro. You don't need to stress over that, right now."

Mo looked at his brother with a look to kill. T Ski stood there not intimidated by the look Mo was giving him.

"What the fuck do you mean I need not to stress over that? That's my son's mother! I don't have any answers for my son when he's asking about his mother! Bella's parents showed up here today, while I was up at the hospital trying to get my son. I thought you would be here. You left out of the house and didn't tell me shit. I wouldn't have gone out, if you weren't going to be here." Mo said with an attitude. "You know that there is always supposed to be a man present in this home or close to home."

"They were good." T Ski dropped the duffel bag that he was holding onto the floor. Mo noticed the bag and gave T Ski a questioning look.

"What's in that bag?" Mo asked.

T Ski looked to his left and saw that Taz B was sitting on the couch, looking in his direction. T Ski lifted the bag up off the floor and motioned for Mo to follow him into his room. Mo got up out of his seat and followed T Ski.

T Ski opened his door and placed the bag on his floor. Mo entered inside the room behind him.

"Close and lock the door." T Ski ordered. Mo complied. T Ski sat down at his computer and turned it on. He reached for the duffel bag and opened it. Mo looked inside of the bag and saw stacks of money. Mo's eyes grew wide, as he looked on in disbelief. "My boys moved K2O over in Brownsville houses yesterday and today. They made $21,000 dollars. There is 24 men or more in each project that's working around the clock. Van Dyke projects is moving quickly. Riverdale is good and so is Howard projects. Each night, there should be close to $50,000 pulled in after the chiefs take their cuts. Some of the projects that I'm targeting are slow, but things will pick up once word gets out about K2O," T Ski said, now typing in a few things on his computer.

"Why do you need so many niggas for each project? Wouldn't it take longer than necessary to pay them all off? You said 6 months bro and you haven't even dominated the other 10 projects in Brownsville. I don't know how this shit is going to work out, but I got a lot of shit going on in my personal life. My baby moms is in the damn hospital. I have my son here with me, not to mention worrying about Mommy. Now, Bella's parents are trying to keep me from her and take my son away from me. Taz B is acting pussy. Tadow and Lee are still bullshittin' out there in the streets, bringing heat to the family. I don't know what the fuck you got planned, Bro. But I know I am starting to get worried." Mo leaned against T Ski's door and rubbed his forehead.

"Mo, things are going to work out. I know what I'm doing," T Ski responded.

"You keep saying you know what you're doing. But you need to explain to me what the fuck is going on! I don't have time to be playing these fucking guessing games with you, man. This shit is starting to fuck with me! Have you taken a look around you to even notice what's been going down? We are doing shit in the hood where we lay our heads. Smart niggas don't do dirt in their own hood," Mo said.

"I have a meeting to go to in a few minutes. I would like for you to accompany me. I have instructions for what is needed and what is to be said. Make sure that your brother isn't planning to go anywhere right now. We need for him to stay behind and keep watch over the house." T Ski said. Before Mo could say anything, T Ski's phone started going off. "Hello," T Ski answered. "Okay that's fine. Thank you." T Ski ended the call.

Mo was wondering what the brief call was about and with whom. He didn't ask. Mo unlocked the door and exited the room. He headed down the hallway and straight to the living room where Taz B was. "Are you going out any time soon?" Mo asked.

Taz B looked up at Mo.

"Why?" Taz B asked with an attitude.

"Listen, we have to run out for a minute and there needs to be a man here at all times," Mo responded.

"I'm getting real sick of you and your brother. Real talk. Ever since you found out this little nigga was a fucking certified genius, you been taking orders from his young ass like he's some kind of king. I don't take orders from no one. This shit he got going on is going to blow up in your face, and I'm not going to be a part of the shit," Taz B remarked.

"Shut the fuck up! I don't take orders from anyone either, but if he has the capability to get our mother well and get us up out of Brooklyn, then I'm all for it. You on the other hand need to learn how to be more supportive of family and stop acting like a pussy. When we first brought the idea to you and told you of T Ski plan, you were down. Now that shit is getting too hot for your ass, you want to bitch up on us. Fuck you, Taz, for real! I don't have time for your shit right now. I need for you to stay here with Mommy, Andrea, and Xavier until we get back. You can do what the fuck you want to do when I get back here," Mo said shaking his head as he went into the kitchen. He understood what Taz B was saying because he felt partially the same way. But as T Ski's big brother, he was going to ride this out to see where this took them.

"Fuck you too, Mo! I don't know why y'all motherfuckers getting all hot over me not wanting to be a part of this shit. Your brother got people everywhere. He's good without me. You calling me pussy and then you should know that I give it up just like the next motherfucker. That's not the life I'm trying to live anymore. This nigga is pumping fucking drugs and making enemies for us all to buy the chemicals he's giving to Mommy in hopes to make her well. Do you really think this shit is for Mommy? And the fucking genius ain't even in school! Why you not down this nigga throat about getting his education? I don't understand you. I don't give a fuck about what you or anyone else thinks about me. I'm not with this shit. I have better shit to do with my life. I guess now is a better time than any to let you know that I'm moving out," Taz B said.

"Where are you going? You know Mommy needs all of us here for her," Mo replied.

"You two motherfuckers aren't worried about Mommy. You out there helping this nigga who is supposed to be a fucking genius sling rocks and take over the fucking projects killing motherfuckers who been doing this shit forever and for what? This nigga T Ski is going to fuck around and get us all killed. I'm not dying over no fucking territory that I can care two fucks about. If T Ski really wanted to help Mommy, then he would take his ass to school and get a degree like we all had to do. Find a good job and help take care of home. He's doing shit right here where we live. How safe are we really, when we live right where the nigga is setting shit off. If he was that fucking smart, then he would get us the hell away from here and do what the fuck he needs to do. You got your fucking son here, but you ain't thinking about his safety either. You are all that boy has right now, but you're out there jeopardizing your life to help your 15 year old brother take over damn near 15 projects, trying to make money. If that's the life you and he want, then more power to you. Don't knock me for wanting better!"

Hearing Taz B, Mo was speechless. The more Taz B spoke, the more sense he made. Now Mo didn't know what to do. He didn't want to get locked up or possible be killed, ultimately leaving his own son behind. Mo cleared his throat as he went into the kitchen and sat down by the window. He stared out into the street at all the people passing by. Xavier couldn't go outside and play now like the normal kids, because Mo was afraid of someone kidnapping or doing bodily harm to his son, just to get back at him. He couldn't go for it. Mo felt bad that since the whole time his sister has been home, she hadn't been anywhere to enjoy herself, because she was confined to their mother's bedside. Mo knew that things had to get better for them all. He didn't want to disappoint T Ski and refrain from covering his back. He wanted to go all the way with his brother because he believed in his heart that T Ski knew what he was doing. It worried Mo sometimes but that was normal. He had been the main male figure in his brother's lives.

Mo tried to come up with something to convince Taz B to stay, but couldn't find the words. Taz B was grown and entitled to make his own decisions. Mo didn't want his brother to leave but knew that there would be no way he could stop him.

Andrea walked into the kitchen and stood by the refrigerator, staring at Mo. "I agree with Taz B. You guys are making me more nervous every time you walk out that door. I know if I'm fearful, imagine what Mommy is feeling. She was up out of the bed yesterday and walking around. I wanted to take her outside to get some fresh air but knew that wasn't possible, because I don't know if there are people out there looking for you all. We can't do shit, because of what's going on outside in the streets. Is this what you guys had in mind to help Mommy? Because it isn't working. All Mommy needs is love and attention from her loved ones. Every day she's doing something different, and you guys are so busy running the fucking streets that none of you even noticed," Andrea stated.

Mo answered, "I don't need this shit right now. I'm getting sick of everyone complaining. I have been there for you all, and now that T Ski has come up with an idea to help us all out of the projects to get a new start, all I'm hearing is bitching. Anything you guys have ever needed or wanted, I was there for you. All I ask is that we give our brother a chance to prove that he will hold good on his word and do what's best for this family. I get scared and concerned, as well, but I trust my brother, and I know that he loves his family. If we don't all work together, then we will never get shit done. The boy is really doing the damn thing, and when shit goes down and he holds good on his promise. Don't be mad if he overlooks those that didn't want no parts of it. I have a son to worry about, but yet I'm out here doing what my brother asks to do. I believe in him, and he hasn't let me down yet. You guys need to chill and have a little faith. If I felt things were getting out of hand, then I would step up and do whatever I had to do to make sure that you all were safe."

Andrea stood with her head held down. She hated to see Mo upset because he had been the father figure in all their lives since Po got locked up. It was Mo money that paid for her to go to college along with her mother's checks. She was truly grateful for a big brother like him.

"I'm sorry Mo. I didn't mean to get you upset. I just don't want to walk outside and get hit by a bullet or anything happen to me because of what you guys are into. I didn't mean no harm," Andrea said softly.

"No one knows that we are behind anything. We are clear Andrea. I'm going to see what I can do about making sure that someone is with you all anytime you want to go out. I don't want you to feel that you can't go outside and walk the streets of Brooklyn because of us. That's not my intentions to have my family living in fear. T Ski and I are going out for a few and I will talk to him about a few things," Mo replied.

T Ski had overheard the whole conversation even the feud between Mo and Taz B. He knew that it was time for him to turn all
the way up, show and prove to his family that he was the man that
everyone was going to envy and want to be like.

"Mo, we need to head out now. Andrea, if you and Mommy want
to go out today, it's perfectly fine. Don't worry about anything happening to you. Let your brother know that he can leave whenever
he's ready. He don't need to stay here any longer than necessary. I
have you all covered." T Ski started toward the door, unlocking it
and exiting the apartment. Mo looked at Andrea and shook his head.
Mo couldn't help but to chuckle because he couldn't believe his little brother was acting like he was the HNIC. Mo stood from his seat
and tried to catch up to T Ski.

Mo knew that T Ski had been acting funny toward Taz B even
Taz had all the right to be mad at him, but Mo didn't like the way T
Ski referred to Taz B, being their brother and not his. Mo knew that
he was going to have to talk to T Ski about what was going on. There
had to be more to this than T Ski was admitting. Either way, Mo was
going to find out and nip shit in the bud. He didn't need his family
becoming rivals. That's not how they were raised, and he wasn't
going to let anything or anyone bring division in his family.

"You know I'm going to ask you about that remark you made back in the house about Taz," Mo said, as both brothers exited the building.

"I'm not about to get into that with you. I have better things on my mind than him," T Ski said, as they walked down the strip leading towards the street. A black Escalade truck pulled up in front, double-parking in the streets. A heavyset guy who was dressed in a black suit jumped out of the front seat and held open the back door of the car. Mo looked around to see who the guy was waiting for but didn't see anyone around. Mo continued to follow T Ski, who walked up to the truck and entered.

Mo paused for a second and took a look at the guy who held the door open. He stared back at Mo but didn't utter a word.

"Are you getting in the car or what? I have moves I need to make," T Ski said.

Mo climbed inside of the truck sitting beside T Ski. He couldn't believe that his baby brother had niggas chauffeuring him around. He wondered where T Ski was getting the money from to pay for such services but knew better than to question his brother around anyone.

Sonovia Alexander

Chapter 16
Langston Hughes Projects
DC

"I have been hearing a lot of shit about these boys from out of town, coming into our projects trying to shut shit down. I'm not having that shit. These motherfuckers had better know that I'm not the one. I will not get caught slipping. Any of you motherfuckers that are feeling threatened, lay that shit out here, right now. Because if any of you come up short on any of my money, you're a done deal!" DC explained, as he blew smoke out of his mouth from his cigar.

"I don't know who the fuck these niggas are. I heard from Dex that these niggas been hitting up the heads and then taking over shit. I know they got Van Dyke, Riverdale, Brownsville Housing, and Tilden on lock. I'm not sure of any of the other projects though. Kirby thinks that those niggas, Tadow and Lee, got something to do with these out of town niggas. They pushing some new shit out there called K2O. Fiends can't get enough of the shit. It's getting to a point that no one will cop from anyone, if they don't have this new shit that's out here. We need to find who their connection is and try to get on. My nigga Rock said the niggas were sizing him up, when he tried to get put on and they brushed the nigga off like he wasn't shit.

These niggas are at least 10 deep. They stay together watching each other's back," Panama explained.

DC didn't like the shit that he had just heard. He was an old timer. He was in his early 50's and had worked his ass off to lock down Langston Hughes, Glenmore, and Plaza projects out here in Brownsville. He wasn't about to lose his money to some young ass niggas that weren't even from Brooklyn.

DC turned and looked at his five top men, all seated in the living room. He knew he was going to have to get all his top dogs out there to set shit off, and let niggas know. If they thought about coming up against him and his soldiers, they would fall.

"I need to know everything about these motherfuckers. Where they are from, who they're working for, and who their supplier is? Get them niggas Cali and Drew on the phone and tell them to get their men out there! I don't want to hear shit about niggas taking over my shit. That's not happening! They got at Big L, that dirty ass nigga Barry, Rant's young ass got it, too, and that other nigga Sugar Foot's pussy ass. From what I'm hearing, these motherfuckers are going after the head niggas, and I'm waiting for one of them motherfuckers to run up on me. If my camp don't make no money out here on these streets, then no motherfucker out here is going to eat! I don't want to hear from any of you motherfuckers unless you got answers for me!" DC shouted and he meant every word he said. DC sent his brother a text and told him that he needed to see him ASAP. He had to make sure that shit was tied up and on lock on his end. He wasn't giving up his spots for no one.

DC and his brother Cruise were products of a pimp and prostitute. When Cash met their mother Donna, he had already made a name for himself in the streets, as being one of the biggest pimps in Brooklyn. Niggas respected his grind, because he had some of the baddest bitches working for him. Cash always showed up to parties in the hood with six of his main bitches. None of the girls ever left one single party without at least a thousand dollars in their pockets. The girls would fuck, suck, lick, or whatever they had to do to make their money. Cash felt like he was a fair pimp, because he gave his hoes half of their money. He made sure that they stayed clean, sexy, and appealing. He housed all 15 of his girls in three apartments in a building in Newport Gardens.

That is where he met and fell for Donna. She had heard about him and tried to stay clear of him not wanting to be turned out like the other women were. He was good looking and had money. Cash had pursued Donna and kept sending her gifts to get in good with her. Donna, had finally broke down and gave in, deciding to go out on a date with Cash. Donna had made it very clear on their date that she would never be a hoe. And if he was going to treat her like one, she wasn't interested. Cash laid down his Mack and fed Donna a bunch of dreams. He did fulfill some of them by buying her a house he promised her and making Donna the mother of his kids. DC was his first born, and then Cruise came along. Donna thought that she and Cash would be married after being together for 5 years but it never happened. Cash was still sleeping with other women, along with his hoes and wasn't ready to settle down. He felt that Donna was being unappreciative after he made sure that she lived a lavish lifestyle.

It wasn't long before Cash had Donna out on the streets working for him, due to her continuous nagging and disrespect. Cash did love her but was completely turned off. After he sent the first John to his house to have his way with Donna, she didn't refuse or put up a fight. She gave in, and Cash knew from that point on that she would never be more than just a hoe who had birthed his two sons. He had hoped that he had a good woman. He would've imagined Donna calling him with panic in her voice letting him know that someone was trying to make a move on her. Cash needed to know if he could really trust her, or if she was just like the same women, he had on the corners. Donna had proven that she was just the same.

Cash stopped doing for Donna and had taken his sons from her, sending them to live with his mother. Donna had gotten hooked on drugs and two years later, when DC was 9 and Cruise 7, they had found out that their mother had died from an overdose. They didn't know how true that was because rumors were floating around that Cash had set Donna up. DC and Cruise were devastated, hearing about the passing of their mother but hadn't really been around her since they were very young, 4 and 2 years of age. They hadn't see her much and didn't hear from her.

Cash wasn't any better. He only came around to drop off money and to make sure that his boys were taken care of. Nothing more.

It wasn't a surprise that DC and Cruise grew up and became pimps, following in their father's footsteps. Being that DC was the oldest, he taught Cruise everything that he had learned from watching other pimps in the street. It wasn't until his early twenty's when DC got into the drug game. He and Cruise had to make a name for themselves, other than just pimping. They started sticking up guys from different projects and taking their work from them to sell to crackheads in their building. Every Friday, DC and Cruise schemed on which project they would hit, steering clear of the old heads who had their turf on lock. It was usually the young hustlers that they hit up, knowing that they would get away with taking their product, without having to watch their backs.

Once DC and Cruise had enough money saved up, they found a supplier that gave them a good price on a kilo of cocaine for $30,000. It had taken them months to save up the money, but DC was determined to be his own boss and have enough money to live good for the rest of his life. He refused to give up. He and his brother didn't have anything else going for them and had to do whatever necessary in order to survive.

DC pulled out his phone and called his best friend James, who held Glenmore down. DC needed to know that all of his men were on point.

"What's good, bro?" James answered.

"I need to see you," DC replied, as he disconnected his call. He grabbed his bottle of Hennessey and took a sip from it, as he waited for his brother and James.

T Ski

"Where are we headed?" Mo asked.

"I have to make a few stops before tonight, Bro. I know that you have questions for me right now, but unfortunately, I can't give you the answers you're looking for. I have a lot of shit going on, and it would take me days to fill you in on everything. Right now, I need for you to just focus on doing as I tell you to do, so we can make shit happen."

Mo didn't like how his brother was talking to him. He was the one who had raised T Ski, not the other way around. Before he could open up his mouth to speak, T Ski's phone started going off.

"Yo," T Ski answered.

"It's taking care of," The caller said.

"Good." T Ski ended the call. He pulled down what Mo hadn't noticed before, a laptop that was installed into the back of the driver's seat. T Ski typed in a few things and waited, as a bunch of information loaded onto the screen. Mo was trying to get a good look at what was displayed on the small device, but from where he was seated, the font was too small for him to make out. Mo looked on as his brother started typing like 100 wpm. Mo didn't know how the hell he could even see those small words on the screen but decided to just focus his attention out of the window. Mo was weary about all the things going on around him. Knowing that his brother was making all this shit happen, gave him a new profound respect for T Ski.

"Pablo, take me to the shop. I need you to get in and out of there. You got twenty minutes to get there and another 5 minutes to get out," T Ski ordered.

"Yes, sir," Pablo answered. Mo wondered what the hell the shop was and what was inside this shop.

Mo spoke up. He couldn't help himself. "I can't help but to think that you been had some of these things you're doing already in motion."

"I did. I'm just bringing you guys into it now. I told you, brother, I got this. You will see what I'm capable of." T Ski closed down the laptop and tucked it away, back into the seat.

Mo sat back without saying another word. He had a feeling that his brother really was nothing to be fucked with, and Mo could only hope that when everything was said and done, they would be able to walk away from this with their lives.

To Be Continued...
Brooklyn On Lock 2
Coming Soon

Coming Soon From Lock Down Publications

GANGSTA CITY

By **Teddy Duke**

A DANGEROUS LOVE **VII**

By **J Peach**

BURY ME A G **III**

By **Tranay Adams**

BLOOD OF A BOSS **III**

By **Askari**

DON'T FU#K WITH MY HEART **III**

By **Linnea**

THE KING CARTEL **II**

By **Frank Gresham**

SILVER PLATTER HOE **II**

By **Reds Johnson**

THESE NIGGAS AIN'T LOYAL **III**

By **Nikki Tee**

BROOKLYN ON LOCK **II**

By **Sonovia Alexander**

THE STREETS BLEED MURDER **II**

By **Jerry Jackson**

DIRTY LICKS **II**

By **Peter Mack**

THE ULTIMATE BETRAYAL **II**

By **Phoenix**

CONFESSIONS OF A DOPEMAN'S DAUGHTER

Sonovia Alexander

By **Rasstrina**

<u>Available Now</u>

LOVE KNOWS NO BOUNDARIES **I & II**

By **Coffee**

SLEEPING IN HEAVEN, WAKING IN HELL **I, II & III**

By **Forever Redd**

THE DEVIL WEARS TIMBS **I, II & III**

By **Tranay Adams**

DON'T FU#K WITH MY HEART **I & II**

By **Linnea**

BOSS'N UP **I & II**

By **Royal Nicole**

A DANGEROUS LOVE **I, II, III, IV, V, VI**

By **J Peach**

CUM FOR ME

An **LDP Erotica Collaboration**

THE KING CARTEL

By **Frank Gresham**

BLOOD OF A BOSS **I & II**

By **Askari**

BURY ME A G **I & II**

By **Tranay Adams**

LOYALTY IS BLIND

By **Kenneth Chisholm**

A HUSTLA'Z AMBITION **I & II**

By **Damion King**

THESE NIGGAS AIN'T LOYAL **I & II**
By **Nikki Tee**
THE STREETS BLEED MURDER
By **Jerry Jackson**
DIRTY LICKS
By **Peter Mack**
THE ULTIMATE BETRAYAL
By **Phoenix**

Sonovia Alexander

BOOKS BY LDP'S CEO, CA$H

TRUST NO MAN
TRUST NO MAN 2
TRUST NO MAN 3
BONDED BY BLOOD
SHORTY GOT A THUG
A DIRTY SOUTH LOVE
THUGS CRY
THUGS CRY 2
TRUST NO BITCH
TRUST NO BITCH 2
TRUST NO BITCH 3
TIL MY CASKET DROPS

Coming Soon

TRUST NO BITCH (EYEZ' STORY)
THUGS CRY 3
BONDED BY BLOOD 2